THROUGH THE EYES
OF THE BEHOLDER

A.S. DRAYTON

Copyright © 2022-2023 by A.S. Drayton (Anthony S. Drayton III)
Published in 2023 by A.S. Drayton Books LLC
All rights reserved. For information about reproducing any
selections from this book, contact
info@asdraytonbooks.com

ISBN 979-8-35090-661-5

Credits
Edited by Charles Stewart
Cover Art by Luce

THROUGH THE EYES OF THE BEHOLDER

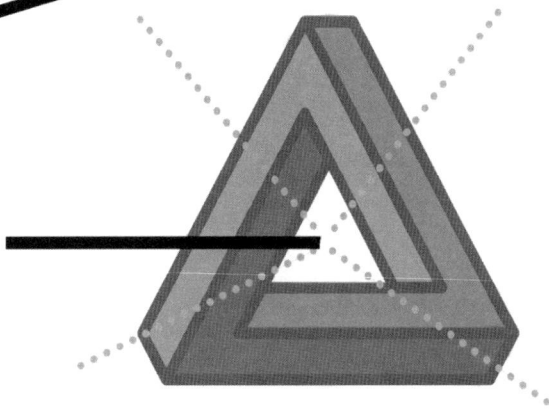

A.S.
DRAYTON

To my loving wife, my wild children, and my supportive family, both those chosen and by blood.

CONTENTS

The Spanish glossary is organized chronologically by Prism and page appearance. To avoid spoilers, try not to look beyond the page you are reading.

THROUGH THE EYES
OF THE BEHOLDER

CURIOUS WHITE STRINGS
BIRTH A NEW SPRING MELODY
AND SHINE OUT THE DARK

PRISM 7

PRIDE AND JOY

RIAN SINGER

Alone, in a humid, pitch-black cavern, Rian Singer finds himself staring at a single, glimmering light in the distance. The atmosphere, thick with moisture and warm as fresh blood, leaves him gasping for air with every step as the ground squishes beneath his feet. He can feel the sweat collecting on his copper-haired brow, until finally dripping down and traveling across his freckled, ivory skin. But the wanderer, hyper-focused on reaching the light, never once wipes the sweat, sensing that if he wastes the energy, his goal and salvation will remain out of reach.

Where am I? The thirteen-year-old wonders desperately as he feels himself ready to collapse on the ground, which seems to pulsate and squirm beneath his bare feet.

But, deeper and deeper he walks, until finally he realizes the light leads not to an exit, but a figure, crouching in the heart of the black abyss. The luminescent figure, too bright to be scrutinized, remains still.

"Help!" Rian screams, feeling relieved at the sight of the angel-like being. A relief that is instantly swallowed by despair.

Ignoring his scream, the figure disappears, leaving nothing but true darkness. Pure black, absent of light. Rian drops to his knees, defeated.

And then, the light returns; its cold rays rain down on his exposed neck. His unprotected skin numbs as the icy beams envelop him.

Relief washes over Rian, his savior having returned. He attempts to turn in gratitude, but fails, finding himself frozen in place and unable to blink.

The brilliance of the figure illuminates the unstable cavern floor beneath Rian, revealing the boy's path to be endless layers of coagulated blood.

Panic seeps into the youth's heart. He is unable to speak, or scream.

A sharp and slender hand, composed of pure light, creeps into view from over the teen's right shoulder. As the hand nears his face, he realizes the light is actually the shine of countless prisms. Prisms that make up the hand's entirety.

Prisms of varying size and thickness, rotating and swarming around one another as if they were not only alive, but sentient, merely imitating the form of a hand.

The pseudo-appendage grips Rian's head, blinding him as the prisms of its palm dance before his aquamarine eyes.

The white-gold rays beaming from the prisms twist into shapes and become tinted with vivid color. Images flood the boy's vision as if the dam separating his memory and reality had been broken.

The first image he sees is the effortless, carefree smile of the self-proclaimed "Heir to The Spirit of Armonia", Nesho White. Nesho is Rian's newly-appointed project partner and, unbeknownst to Nesho himself, Rian's intellectual rival. A cheeky wall of luck and intellect that Rian could never seem to best in spite of his best efforts.

"Hey Rian, we should be partners! Us bleeding hearts should stick together, y'know? A partnership of the two smartest kids in class would make this assignment a cake walk." He declares with his pearly whites bare. "I'm thinking we could do our report on indigenous Mexican culture. I've got a pretty good source!"

Why didn't I say anything? Why did I concede to that stupid grin? Why can't I smile, and share my opinions, like him? The jealous teen questions. *Father would never...*

Immediately, at the very thought of his father, the prisms' momentum quickens and the colors bleeding into the boy's vision shift drastically. Rian sees none other than himself, seated before him in the dining room chair.

The cruel, chilling voice of his father forces itself from his own lips. "At this rate, the boy will never be enough." With a will of its own his head tilts downward, and Rian notices his right arm is now scar ridden like his father's. He can feel his own face twist into a grimace as the fingers clench and the arm shakes from frustration, becoming the same disappointed gaze that graced his father's face and dampened every morning of Rian's existence for as long as he could remember.

As the teen's eyes roll into the back of his head, a final set of images reaches his mind. A shed the size of a three-car garage, crowned with a simple metal roof supported by walls painted like rust-colored adobe - his father's workshop. There was a singular door on the windowless wall facing the house, a door only his father could enter via a keypad nestled to the right of the doorway.

No matter how much I've helped him, no matter how hard I work, he's always loved his glorified shed more than me. His pride and joy. Rian thinks at the sight of the only recipient of his father's smile.

The luminescent prisms continue to swirl chaotically as the creature's grip tightens; the boy can feel as they ravenously slice his eyelids and streams of ruby pour down to cloud his vision.

The sensation leaves the teen free of thought; with no energy or will to fight the inevitable. Feeling at peace as his consciousness fades, Rian finally relinquishes himself to his fate.

That is, until he hears an abrupt crash, like glass shattering and clanging against the floor. Without warning or pause, the prisms vanish, and the light with it.

Yet, the teen is not left in darkness. A dim light shines from above.

Rian, able to move once more, looks up to see an opening where the roof of the cavern once was. An opening that shows not the sky, but the ceiling of his bedroom.

As the young man continues to stare at the strange phenomenon, he slowly realizes he is awake and lying in his bed.

Rian touches his face as if to confirm the cuts from the prismatic creature's fragmented palm had all been a dream. Relieved, the youth lets out the breath he had been holding in his sleep, and gasps for air.

That carefree mop is even giving me nightmares now. I can't believe Ms. Hughes agreed with Nesho and thought it was a good idea to pair us up. Rian drags his hand down his face, lamenting his forced truce with his oblivious nemesis.

Whether it's schoolwork, chess, or a game of Civ, he trumps me. Rian laments. *My only hope is robotics, but there's no way for me to show off since Dad keeps everything in his shed. I need to find a way to outshine him. If I can't do that, winning Dad's approval may as well be a pipe dream.* The boy's thoughts refocus on himself, as he notices a growing chill spreading over his body.

After patting his clothes, it becomes obvious they are drenched with sweat.

Rian haphazardly tosses off his soaked clothes and throws on a pair of navy-blue gym shorts that he blindly pulls out of the drawer next to his bed. With a half- yawn-half-sigh, he slides off his mattress and heads to the bathroom for a drink of water to replenish his body, closing the door behind him softly.

As he passes the railing that borders the stairway, located to the left of his bedroom door, the boy hears the muffled squeak of a chair and broken glass cracking beneath someone's feet.

That's strange. Dad must have dropped something. Rian thinks. Looking to his right and down the short hall, the teenager sees his father's bedroom door, wide open. The motionless room is covered in shadows, lit only by the weak, amber glow from the alarm clock resting on his father's nightstand. The boy chuckles as he steps into the bathroom on the opposite side of the hall from his own room. The mental picture of his astute and serious father suffering a nightmare as well and hightailing it downstairs was a brief oasis of joy.

Rian continues into the bathroom and turns on the light. Then, out of habit, he ambles over to the small window at the back of the bathroom to gaze at his father's workshop behind the house. The workshop was nearly invisible, surrounded by the all-consuming darkness that easily devoured his home - a secluded place surrounded by the wilderness of Otay Mesa, California. Only the scarlet light of the shed's keypad, fixed into those venerated walls, next to the entrance betrayed its existence.

Why does he always work so late? Rian wonders, scratching his red hair in thought. As a stray lock falls into his vision, Rian bites down on his bottom lip, pivots toward the mirror and turns on the faucet. As the water flows, the youth stares into the eyes of his own reflection and repeats a single phrase: "I want to study The Celts." Rian murmurs with greater indignation at each repetition, his aquamarine eyes shining like blue flames.

Dad wouldn't have buckled when Nesho said he wanted to study Mexican culture, and I shouldn't either! Rian shouts in his head, until shame reclaims the teen as he notices the brilliance of his own irises, and he lowers his head.

What color are Nesho's eyes? He ponders, before sucking his teeth, realizing the truth. "I wouldn't know, I don't even have the courage to look him in the eyes." Rian whispers to himself, watching the water flow and funnel down the drain, in a trance.

Then, a creak from the stairs awakens Rian from his trance. He cups some water, throws it down his gullet, shuts off the faucet, and begins heading back to his room.

As he passes through the threshold of the door, he waves to the six-foot-tall silhouette that was nearing the top of the staircase. "Goodnight, Dad." The teen yawns as he steps past the father-like figure and continues toward his bedroom.

As he reaches for the doorknob, he feels a hand rest on his head. Before he can say a word, the hand grips his copper hair like a vice, and a knife is brandished before his eyes.

"Quédese quieto." The assailant grunts.

Thunderstruck, Rian instinctively follows the demands and remains stiff as a board. Tears fill his eyes, as his nightmare comes to life.

"Why?" the youth meekly squeaks; not directing his question at his attacker, but at the universe.

As Rian's eyes close, night-hidden tears run down his freckled cheeks, falling off the stubble of his chin. *Why? Why? Why? Why? Why?* The teen screams in his head, deaf to the world around him.

Then, unexpectedly, the grip loosens, and a harsh thud brings an end to his interrogation of fate. Rian slowly turns, and his aqua eyes rush to bring the intruder into focus. As his vision adjusts, he expects to see vicious greed or murderous intent in his aggressor's glare, but, to his surprise, all he finds in the carob eyes of his assailant are fear and sadness. The eyes of failure. Eyes that the young man knows all too well.

EMMANUEL OSORIO MÉNDEZ

"¿Qué...qué pasó? stammers Emmanuel as he peers back at the copper-headed youth standing before him, still as a squirrel assessing its surroundings.

"No puedo mover las piernas o los brazos. No me los puedo sentir." he stutters to himself, as all four of his limbs refuse to move at his command. Emmanuel's vision becomes blurry as a sudden, sharp pain at the back of his skull threatens to whisk him from consciousness, but the boy's visage never leaves his sight.

Debe de ser el hijo del diablo. He thinks, recognizing the boy's signature red hair. *Si lo hubiera atrapado, podría haberla resca..*

The man's regretful notion is interrupted by a towering silhouette with a fiery, auburn mane creeping into his vision.

"I'm glad to see you're okay." the silhouette states calmly. "Did he hurt you at all?"

The boy remains unblinking, incapable of tearing his sight away from the man collapsed on the floor before him, and Emmanuel in turn can't seem to avert his gaze either.

"Who...Who is he?" the shaken teen stammers.

The man peers out the corner of his eye, revealing his piercing blue irises that appear to glow in the shadows as they trace over the incapacitated intruder.

"I have no idea." Declares the man, as he reaches down and presses his finger through a red-stained tear in the right-side of Emmanuel's brown sweater. Emmanuel writhes and opens his mouth to scream, but only a weak moan escapes.

"Luck must have been on your side, Rian. He seems to have collapsed from blood loss." The man reports aloud. "He also doesn't seem to be a thief, either, considering he grabbed you right away and made no attempt to hide or steal anything from downstairs."

The man rises to face the boy, "Between that, the desperate look on his face, and his mumblings, my guess is he's some poor, desperate illegal that someone roped into their scheme. Someone who knows who I am, or who I work for, perhaps? Most likely a competitor of *Davy-Swan* trying to stifle the company's progress by threatening the source of its recent innovations."

Though his vision is fogged, Emmanuel recognizes the hauntingly indifferent demeanor. "Diablo," he mutters to himself.

Emmanuel can only lie in horror, watching the devilish figure kneel again and straighten his limp body. One of The Devil's arms is placed under Emmanuel's knees as the other disappears behind his back.

"Tell no one about this and go to bed. I'll handle the rest." The Devil commands the boy. But the boy remains, frozen. "Trust your father, Rian." The Devil chimes, feigning an affectionate tone that even the dazed Emmanuel could see through.

After the reassuring message, the boy turns and runs to his room, slamming the door shut and leaving Emmanuel and The Devil, who lifts the broken man as if he were a child. Emmanuel's head falls back during the ascent, giving him full view of where he had laid. Blood that had leaked from the poorly bound injury on his right abdomen pooled in narrow cracks between wooden tiles, and a thin red splotch adorned the wall where Emmanuel's head collided with its surface - from it, a single trickle of blood led to the floor.

Emmanuel struggles to keep his thoughts straight as he is whisked down the stairs and lectured in a language made up of words he understands, but whose meaning he fails to comprehend in his growing daze.

"Do you believe you're lucky, or cursed, my friend?" The Devil questions. He allows a brief silence, seemingly awaiting a response, but continues when none is received. "You found my home and broke in while I was in my workshop. You managed to grab my son, securing a hostage. You were so close. You may have actually succeeded, if it weren't for you collapsing to the floor, before achieving anything." The Devil croons.

Immobile, Emmanuel half listens to the endless ramblings of his captor as he watches scenery pass behind him, mapping out his future escape: White stairs capped with wooden tiles that descend to a central hall. A doorway opposite the stairs that leads directly into an oddly clean, meticulously organized kitchen. The kitchen then gives way to a simple white door, which shuts behind them with a heavy slam.

"¿Adónde me lleva?" Emmanuel interrupts weakly yet firmly, tired of the demon's trifles.

"Oh, he speaks?" The Devil mocks as he adjusts his right arm, twisting Emmanuel's head in the process and allowing his injured captee to witness his right hand, riddled with deep hash marks in the skin, tapping on a number pad with a scarlet glow. Following the final tap, a boom is heard, and the door unseals, swinging open to reveal a seemingly endless abyss. Blinding lights then spring to life, purging the room of shadows, and revealing the innards of the mysterious shed.

"¿Qué demonios?" Emmanuel spits, his eyes open wide at the assortment of bestial and humanoid robotic limbs that litter the walls, all plugged into wires that run in between them. Trailing the grid of wiring with his eyes, Emmanuel notices they all originate from the same hole located in the middle of the back wall. In the center of the space stands a modest black desk with two screens and a computer resting on its surface. Two long, silver tables, with drawers facing toward the entrance, flank the desk. On the right table, a metallic-brown hawk sits motionless. On the left, a robotic, skeletal dog whose mouth lies agape, revealing a silver gun barrel where a tongue should be.

The fog of his mind does not stop Emmanuel from stammering at the sight before him.. He looks away from The Devil's familiar hound, and his eyes dart around the room desperately. *Malena. Mi vida. Debes estar aquí.* The man declares in silence, sensing that the love of his life must be hidden in this shed, no bigger than a three-car garage. Despite his position, his plans to escape with his beloved Malena have not changed. He will find a way. Some way; somehow.

The Devil hums whimsically as he places Emmanuel on the cold, metal floor, facing the legs of the desk, and even more wires that bore into the ground. "You know, despite what you may think, I'd say you're pretty lucky. Even that boy of mine hasn't been down here." Emmanuel hears the demon proclaim as a thunderous pang blares from the floor and he feels it begin to vibrate against his skull. The workshop, what he thought would be his final resting place, ascends, leaving him and with it all hope of escape. As he watches the workshop rise, and feels his body fall, he can only assume Hell itself is waiting at the bottom of this descent. *He venido al infierno.* Thinks the quickly fading Emmanuel. *Pero lo haría mil veces, si pudiera rescatarla.*

Hell is at least ten times the size of the shed above, a perfect subterranean cube lit by the back wall comprised of sixteen screens and a long, black desk seated beneath them that runs the entire length. Underneath the desk, rests a single, meshed work chair. Emmanuel is able to make out a large vat on the right side of the room, halfway between himself and the screens; stacks of canisters labeled "KOH" stand tall on both of its sides. On the opposite side of the room, Emmanuel notices a small operating room surrounded by glass walls and filled with pristine white equipment that reflect sapphire rays projecting from the rotating Penrose triangles on the screens. In the center of the operating room, at the foot of a surgical bed, stands a metallic demon. Six, silver, crab-like legs join at a central matte-black column. Toward the top of its central column extended four lanky, humanesque arms at each cardinal direction; like petals of a former bud that gives life to the flower of needle-like appendages, adorned with filled syringes and surgical blades, that crown the top of the creature.

With a clap from the devilish showman, lights on the ceiling flash on and a white, tiled floor spanning the entirety of the dungeon is revealed.

"Up we go." The Devil sings as they reach the bottom, and Emmanuel's head eases back from the oddly careful lift-and-turn as The Devil circumvents the computer desk. In that moment, behind the elevator pad, Emmanuel sees a glass barrier, made up of metal support frames and glass panes thicker than those used for the operating room, barring off an area whose length runs that of Hell's, but was no wider, nor taller than a jail cell. "¿Emmanuel?" a familiar voice cries to the immobile hostage. "¡Emmanuel!" The voice yells louder, accompanied by a woman's figure running against the glass, finally breaking through the fog that had overcome Emmanuel. Their eyes meet as his vision clears, for but a moment, and the husband smiles, finally reunited with his wife's resplendent copper eyes.

"Malena, lo siento mi vida."

MALENA ZÁRATE IGNACIO

"Todo esto es culpa mía." Malena's ears barely manage to grasp, straining to hear her husband's whispers through the tiny air holes in the glass wall between them.

"Nada es culpa tuya, viejo." Malena sweetly reassures her husband who, as always, blames himself. "Todo va a salir bien, ya verás. No te preocupes."

Malena's face twists as she turns her attention to the ember-maned brute holding her husband. "Padraig, please, let him go!" the woman begs, "You said I was perfect. Aren't I enough?"

Perplexed, Padraig looks down at Emmanuel. "If I let him go, he'll die. Besides, he came all this way for you. How could I not reward such bravery?" Padraig mulls aloud as he turns away and carries Emmanuel off to the operating room.

"Then again, maybe I shouldn't be encouraging failure. He did collapse from his wounds and break his neck when it mattered most, after all."

"Let him go!" Malena screams louder, with a ferocity that causes Padraig to pause momentarily. His only response, a slight chuckle before continuing onward, leaving Malena to watch the back of her captor, inching further away.

Malena runs to the left side of her prison, never allowing the pale and weakened Emmanuel to leave her sight. Stopping in front of a locked door that leads to another sectioned-off area filled with exercise equipment, Malena begins to incessantly bang her fists against the bullet proof slab; tears stream down her face as she watches her husband be thrown onto a table, disrobed, and hooked up to a bag of blood Padraig pulled out of a storage unit in the surgical room.

"Why are you doing this?" Malena yells, her voice cracking from anger. But Padraig, focused on repairing the body before him, leaves her question unanswered. Malena's protests continue for what feels like hours, until all her might is spent. With her knuckles raw and her voice pushed to the brink of death, she collapses to her knees, looks to the ceiling, and sobs silently.

"Finally, a chance to speak," Malena hears emanating from the speaker above her head. "This man truly brought you to life. Who would have thought such fight was behind that unrefined, golden beauty. You two certainly make quite the spirited couple. I'm glad you both survived the H-R field test."

Malena remains kneeling, grinding her teeth at the backhanded compliments as she lowers her gaze back to Padraig and her husband.

"To answer your initial question, upstairs, I make toys and program artificial intelligence for the masses to enjoy, and abuse. Self-driving cars, more efficient batteries, simple robots, weapons, etc. All things those with disposable cash are willing to buy, funding my more ambitious work down here. Here, I develop the tools that will truly elevate humanity. Think fully functional, robotic prosthetics. Mechanical eyes that function like, no better than, your own. Imagine surpassing those bindings of weakness that make you human and breaking the yoke of mortality."

Yoke of mortality? Elevate humanity? Qué locura. ¿Qué tiene que ver? Malena wonders, her eyes unblinking as Padraig ties up the final suture, takes some scissors, and snips away the excess thread. Then Padraig glances over at her through the corner of his eye.

"All that, my dear…Malena, was it? All that you, Emmanuel, and many others have, and will, help me to achieve." Padraig carefully injects Emmanuel's neck with a large, mysterious syringe. He then rises from the stool next to the surgical table, removes his gloves, picks up a second syringe from the storage closet, and exits the room, leaving Emmanuel alone and unconscious. With Padraig out of her way, Malena can now see Emmanuel's chest rising and falling, providing her a modicum of relief.

¡Menos mal! Malena thinks, before realizing the doctor that patched him up was strolling in her direction. Malena jumps to her feet and retreats to the back wall of her prison, her face turned away from the devilish inventor.

Padraig lets out a deep sigh, disappointed in her reaction to his approach. "Humans always fear and demonize what they don't understand; even when it's beneficial for them." He scoffs. "Anyway, this syringe contains a chip that was designed for monitoring vitals, but in your case it will serve as a tracking device of sorts, for insurance purposes."

Malena is perplexed, but intrigued by his statement, and her face softens. "Tracking?" The woman echoes as she looks down at the floor pensively. "So, you are going to let us go?" The woman asks, still staring at the white floors of her prison, denying her captor's gaze and watching his feet.

"Maybe. It all depends on you. Your husband put quite the scare in my son; one I'm sure will stick with him for life." Padraig says. He then pauses for a moment before continuing in Malena's native language.

"Lo que estoy a punto de pedirte es muy importante. ¿mejor que hable español yo?" Padraig questions seriously.

Defiantly, Malena remains silent; her resolve to never speak to the demented tinkerer in her mother tongue obvious.

Padraig sighs once more. "I guess English will have to do then. Despite your mute behavior through the night, you seem to speak it well enough" he declares. Padraig clears his throat and states calmly, with not a shred of doubt or hesitation.

"You have three days to kill my son."

Malena jerks up in disbelief, baffled by the notion. But before she can form a proper thought, she is left speechless by two pools of steely azure staring back at her.

PADRAIG

"Succeed before my son's birthday, Monday morning, and my experiments on your husband will come to a close. And, of course, I won't bother you for the rest of your lives." Padraig asserts.

"But...but why" stammers the alluring subject. "Your own son?"

"An explanation would serve neither you nor me. Your husband's failed rescue mission simply sparked an idea, one I'd like to test." states the genius matter-of-factly, while approaching the stunned Malena and brandishing the second syringe. "Just know, my experiments will not be delayed. They will not end as long as my son still breathes. The longer you take, the less of your husband you'll get back by the end of it."

Padraig towers over the 5'5" Malena as she mentally juggles the facts presented to her. *Just a little bit more should do it.* Padraig thinks as he watches the woman's cinnamon-brown eyes dart between her husband and Padraig's entertained smile, clearly avoiding his hypnotic, sapphire eyes.

"No need to decide now. I only have room here for one subject at a time, and I can come find you whenever I wish. You have three days, so use them wisely." He concludes as he grabs the girl's shoulder with his left hand and flips her around, pressing her against the cold cement back wall. He proceeds to inject the chip near the base of her skull with the accuracy of a sniper.

Padraig lets go of Malena immediately following the quick procedure, and the sobbing test-subject sprints straight out of the prison door. Her ill-planned attempt to reach her husband quickly fails as she runs around the computer desk at the center of the elevator pad and trips.

"¡Viejo! ¡Emmanuel!" The desperate wife cries out, crawling in prone toward her unconscious husband.

Padraig rolls his eyes as he approaches the spirited test subject, too weak from the long night and lack of food to reach her husband. *All these theatrics are putting me behind schedule.* He thinks. Padraig steps on Malena's left ankle, holding her in place. *At least she had the courtesy to take herself to the pad.*

"Remain still." He orders, pressing his left thumb against the power button on the computer. "Oh, Arachne, please begin analysis of subject 160 and preparation for OI and SCI procedures." The doctor shouts as the cell door shuts, and the sixty-foot column of steel beneath them ascends, lifting the platform with it and blocking the door to the subject quarters. Padraig's robotic assistant springs to life. Tiny bulbs on her joints shine blue and her matte torso elongates, revealing her monstrously wide form, and height of ten feet.

"Stop. Please. Padraig." Malena whimpers as one of Padraig's first creations scuttles toward Emmanuel, using two of its hands, and a knife from the bouquet of surgical tools, to strip him of his remaining clothes. Padraig can't help but smile when he sees Malena's palms start to bleed, as the nails of her clenched fists dig into the skin. Then, as her body begins to shake from what he can only assume is hate, Padraig hears something that fills him with a joy he hasn't felt since being acknowledged by the eccentric, but brilliant, Dr. Huygens. The hum of the elevator nearly covers it, but he manages to make out the ire-filled, murderous pledge. "Lo mataré, viejo."

Padraig's heart begins to pump as if he were a love-struck adolescent sitting next to his crush. *Perfect.* He thinks as he licks his lips. His elation is only interrupted as they reach the main floor of the workshop. "It's time to get up." He informs the seething Malena.

"What are you going to do to Emmanuel?" Malena asks between her teeth, begrudgingly standing as commanded.

Padraig sighs, cracking his neck and walking past her toward a set of coat hooks next to the door. "If you mean in general, you already have your answer, but if you're asking about my more immediate plans, you should be able to guess from the surgical-site marks on your eye."

"Now, put this on." Padraig orders, removing an olive green jacket from a hook and tossing it to the distracted Malena. As she hesitantly grazes the black marks around her left eye with the tips of her fingers, the jacket lands on her head and covers her like a veil. "Can't have you drawing any attention with those ripped and bloody clothes."

Malena scoffs at the order but slips on the jacket, throwing the hood over her curly, mocha hair and tucking back all but the strands covering her left eye.

Padraig opens the door for her and gestures her out with a smile. Malena obeys the unspoken direction, but stops and looks back at the elevator pad masquerading as a meager floor beneath a desk. Her eyes then trail to the robotic animals on the silver tables, and then to the robotic limbs on the walls of the workshop.

"Well, this is where we part ways, my friend." Padraig states while nudging Malena through the door unceremoniously. "I wish you all the luck."

Quickly, Padraig turns and allows the door to shut. Dragging himself over to the center of the workshop, he takes a seat at the bolted chair in front of the computer desk. He checks his watch, and sighs. *It's already 6:20 am; The Sun will be up soon. Tonight's events have put me a day behind schedule,* the unrested tinkerer notes, *but it may have just put me one step closer to usurping that unageing man-child.*

Padraig reaches for the keyboard and the computer screen lights up. "The day I no longer have to report to this onyx-haired bastard can't come soon enough." he whispers to himself as he initiates a video call with the only mind he considers, potentially, as great as his own.

After a single ring, the sound stops, and a black lens bordered with a golden-triangle frame fills the screen. ["Hello my dear boy! I feared something may have happened. It's not like you to report late. Did something go wrong with the surgery?"] a voice zealously inquires with a peculiar, otherworldly timbre highlighting every word.

Padraig's right eye twitches in annoyance. "Please back up from the camera, Doctor."

["Why would I want to do that? I'm getting a good look at my favorite child! And I'm loving that new gleam in your eyes!"] The voice declares enthusiastically. ["By the way, if you're not going to call me father, dad, daddy, or any of the such, I'd ask you to respect me by not calling me by my first name."]

"You've changed your name yet again, father?" Padraig concedes with a questioning tone.

The lenses pull back, revealing a man wearing an ivory-gold, laced suit with a matching top-hat, reclining back in his chair. A well-trimmed, midnight beard covers the bottom half of the man's face, permitting only his smooth cheeks, sharp nose and soft hands to expose his youthful, olive skin.

["The title of doctor was too pretentious without the academic credentials to back it up, but I just love the ring of it. So, as of last night, I am now Doctor Peter Huygens."] The eccentric proclaims.

"So, to confirm, your forename is now 'Doctor'?" Padraig asks, already knowing the unfortunate answer. His question, in turn, is met with rapid nods. He sighs once more, and moves on to his report.

"Well, father, subject 159's eye replacement surgery has been delayed for now, but after some unexpected circumstances involving a survivor from the Hawk-Retriever Testing, a more suitable test subject has replaced her. This subject, 160, is a quadriplegic with a damaged spinal cord that will allow for more intraspinal neural-link testing, as well as all previous prosthetic and nano testing meant for 159. Arachne is currently preparing for both procedures to commence promptly upon my return to the lab this afternoon." Padraig reports, ignoring the crestfallen twist of the newly, self-christened Mr. Huygens' lips.

["You're no fun. Always straight to business."] bemoans Padraig's sole benefactor, and his only family beyond his son. [Well, continue. What of 159?"] Huygens asks with a disinterested handwave, looking away from the camera in a huff.

"She has been chipped and released for the time being. I'll be able to recollect her when need be. Considering she is an illegal immigrant with nowhere to go, I'm certain my identity, location and association with your *Davy-Swan* company are safe."

["Well, you've never failed me before, so that's delightful to hear."] Huygens says, playing with his own luxuriant beard. ["Assuming there's nothing more, I'll leave you to a good day's rest. I look forward to tomorrow's report. I'm certain it will be damn good, I can see it in your eyes."] A mischievous grin radiates across his face, and rows of glimmering porcelain-white teeth peek through the hairs of his beard. Without a word more, the screen goes dark as Doctor Peter Huygens ends the call.

Furrowing his brow, the exhausted Padraig stands and turns to leave his workshop but stops at the exit. *Ever the*

perceptive one, Doctor, sensing my glee from across the globe.
Padraig muses as he covers his right eye with his palm.. *I'll have to temper my excitement, before he catches on.*

Truthfully, Padraig knows well that, far beyond his bountiful resources, his adoptive father's greatest strengths were his cunning, strategic mind, and a wisdom that his eccentricity and youthful appearance belied. If Padraig didn't tread carefully, his hopes of surpassing the only god he deemed worthy of reverence, or fear would be dashed. If a plot against such a being were to be discovered, it meant damnation. It meant imprisonment and enslavement. Returning to the hopelessness of his youth is unthinkable, so caution is of the utmost importance.

Finally stepping out of the workshop, the genius walks back into his home and sits at the table in the dining room. He glances over the shattered window of the living area directly across from him, the shards of glass glistening with the morning light. Hearing his son getting ready for school upstairs, Padraig smiles at his luck and the inspiration Emmanuel gifted him.

Test subject 0, the boy born with my genes. I had hoped that permitting him to attend school and view the world for what it truly is would motivate him and drive his learning in the workshop to new heights, but it becomes clearer every day that the process has been ineffective. If I want him to reach for that immortal king's throne and stand at my side as we push humanity to its precipice, I need to erase that boy's weakness and indecision.

Padraig solemnly declares. *Malena, play your part, and, if the boy survives his trial, he will too.*

Peering down at his right hand, plastered with interwoven, cross-shaped scars that extended under the cuff of his light blue shirt, the man whispers, "Even the best metals require refining flames to transform into proper weapons, don't they father?" Suddenly, like fresh whips striking from the past, a sting surges from his hand and up his arm, causing Padraig to wince. But then the inventor grins appreciatively, as if the pain were an old relative; annoying but loved.

Hearing his son tread down the stairs and amble past the kitchen, the man turns his attention to the entryway of the home as his son reaches the door. "Leaving for school so early?" He questions.

"I couldn't sleep, so I woke up Lati and we cleaned up the blood on the stairs and left the knife on your nightstand." The boy announces, placing his hand on the doorknob and staring nervously ahead. "Lati is rinsing out the bucket now and should be down soon to make you breakfast."

Latona, or Lati as Rian lovingly calls her, is Padraig's favorite brainchild. Lati handles maintenance, cooking, and childcare within the home. A soon-to-be father at the time of her creation, Padraig had chosen the form of an entrancing, curly-haired brunette with ochre skin for the base of her design. From her appearance and movement to her motherly personality and speech, everything about her was so human that even Rian believed her to be his mother until he was four years old. Given her apparent free will and ability to improvise, it was no surprise; the only clue to her true nature was, and still is, the silvery, Penrose triangle irises that graced her eyes.

"Understood. But why did you help? There was no need, Latona can handle the work on her own." Padraig investigates further.

"I know, helping just gave me something to do so my mind wouldn't race. Plus, now the work is done, and you'll be able to eat and get some rest sooner." Rian responds.

Padraig grunts and scratches his temple with his index finger. "Some rest would be nice, but I'll be spending the day upping the security around the home." The drained Padraig pronounces as he places his elbows on the table and rests his chin on his interlocked hands. "On a related note, though I doubt anyone would be bold enough to strike in a public space, be careful when you're out in town or at school. The intruder himself seems to have been an unwilling pawn in someone's else's game, but there's no question that someone is targeting us at the moment."

The young man remains pensive, his hand trembling as it grips the doorknob, lost in his own thoughts. "Dad," the boy hesitates for a moment, taking a deep, emboldening breath. "What did you do with the man? I saw him leave your workshop this morning before the sun came up."

Always watching through your little window. Good. Padraig thinks as a sly grin crosses his face. "I merely patched up his wounds. Over the course of the night, I determined he himself wouldn't be a threat in the future. It only felt right to show him some mercy."

But Rian, who at first seems relieved by the news, tenses up moments later. His hand tremors, becoming a vice on the doorknob. No doubt, flashes of shadowy assailants behind every corner must be bombarding his mind. *Perfect.*

Padraig stands up and walks over to his son, placing his hand on his shoulder. "You are my son, and one day you will be my partner in the workshop, as we change this world. You will join me as one of the minds that fuel *Davy-Swan*, the technological giant that is quickly eclipsing the competition, thanks to my unparalleled innovations. A few enemies are bound to pop up every now and again, unfortunately. It's human nature to fight such grand change."

Padraig fakes the warmest smile he can, as his son looks back at him with tears welling in his aquamarine eyes. "As always, I'll do all I can to keep you safe, but I can't be everywhere. Be smart, stay safe, and get ready to help your old man transform this world into a better place." The genius says, calling his son to action; pushing him toward the destiny Padraig had planned for him long ago.

RIAN SINGER

Though Rian's worries evaporate at his father's request, tears still cloud his vision. He looks away, embarrassed by his own emotions, and nods enthusiastically while wiping the crystalline drops before they can fall. But, the battle was lost the moment his father's words of encouragement flowed, and the gentle teen is left with one choice if he wants to save face; run out the door. Rian does just that, waving at his father and then hopping into the backseat of the Abeona v.1.

Abby, as Rian affectionately dubbed her, is an unassuming, green sedan powered by a voice-commanded, self-driving AI his father recently programmed; a prototype for a project meant to eliminate the need for human drivers altogether. Rian's father even predicted that driver's licenses would become obsolete once she was complete, only seeing use by the old guard who would rather drive the sentimental relics that gave them a sense of control.

He believes in me. Rian repeats in his head the entire trip as Abby chauffeurs him from the outskirts of Otay Mesa, to Armonia School in the city of Chula Vista; the recent memory of his father's smile like honey on his lips. *I won't let him down. I can't.*

Invigorated, Rian jumps out of Abby the moment she comes to a halt in front of the Armonia School building, and before Abby can so much as shut her door and turn back for home, Rian disappears into a crowd of students.

Shoving past his peers that were gathered near the entrance and barging through the doors, Rian picks up his pace with every step. His mind focused on one goal; to find Nesho White.

"No running in the halls!" Rian hears a teacher yell, but he ignores them without so much as a glance. Undeterred, the teen continues until he feels himself grabbed by the collar. With too much momentum Rian fails to stop on a dime, and he hears a staggered yelp from behind as another hand grasps his left shoulder.

"Did you not hear me?" blares the voice of his homeroom teacher, Ms. Hughes, clearly annoyed by the hurried youth's mad dash as she regained her balance. "I know I'm not the biggest woman in the world, but you nearly dragged all one hundred seventy pounds of me down the hall like a baby."

She lets go of his collar and Rian turns to face her with nervous laughter, slightly ashamed, as he looks down at the ground.

"Sorry Ms. Hughes, I wasn't thinking." He stutters, embarrassed with himself.

"What kind of apology is that Mr. Singer?" the school-wide-favorite teacher interjects. "Look someone in the eyes when you apologize and say what you're sorry for."

Rian blushes, but does as the teacher asks, "I'm sorry for running in the halls and nearly knocking you over, Ms. Hughes!"

THELA HUGHES

I wonder what has this kid all fired up this morning. He's usually so docile. Thela thinks, still catching her breath from the brief shock but standing tall above her student. *And how did he do that? What is he? Like 5'4?*

"Very good. Now, where are you even running off to, our classroom is back that way." Thela asks, pointing two doors down the hall.

Rian nervously plays with his fingers, a return to his normally squirrely self. He parts his lips to respond, but he is quickly interrupted by another of Thela's students.

"Never seen you so spirited before!" Thela hears the cheerful, and unmistakable voice of Nesho White sing. She watches him stroll up to Rian, wearing the same zip-up, platinum hoodie that she told him to remove dozens of times in the past. For some reason, Nesho seemed proud of the garb that clashed with the school's uniform, yet shone like a holy cloak against his caramel skin and dark, loose curls that fell to his shoulders. The mere sight of the onyx number one sewn into the right breast causes Thela to roll her eyes, knowing she'd have to regurgitate the same speech that would fall on deaf ears. But, before a word can leave her lips, Nesho pats Rian on the back, causing Rian to jump and spin to face him.

"What's gotten into you?" Nesho asks the normally inoffensive and hushed red head.

"I want to do our presentation on The Celts!" Rian yells without warning, surprising none more than his homeroom teacher, Thela Hughes. "For our history project." he continues, now slightly flustered but still obstinate. "I want to study The Celts."

Thela titters to herself and briefly flashes an amused grin. *So, that's what this is all about?*

Nesho stares in disbelief for a few seconds, but then brandishes his signature, pearly grin that puts the glow of his dress code violation to shame. "Sure, you seem awfully passionate. I don't mind switching our topic if Ms. Hughes says it's okay."

Suddenly, what sounds like a small army slamming lockers in unison breaks out from down the hall, distracting Thela as she scrutinizes the sea of youths adorned in dark blue shirts and khaki, to no avail. Irritated by the rambunctious morning, she closes her eyes and sighs in preparation to find the source of the noise. *Why today? Can't we all just cruise into the weekend?* She thinks, rubbing her temples.

"As long as I get no more trouble out of you today, that's fine by me." Thela finally answers as she walks past Rian and Nesho, starting her hunt for the zealous racket down the hall.

Then, as Thela shuffles through the youth-laden hall, the roar of Rian's celebratory outburst reaches her ears, and a powerful grin pokes through her frustration once more.

Finally speaking his mind, Thela thinks as she follows the metallic echoes, *how could I not encourage that?*

PRISM 6

THE HADA OF CHULA VISTA

THELA HUGHES

Thela begrudgingly saunters down the hall, toward the booms and metal clangs emanating from around the corner. With each step toward the bend in the hall, her pace grows slower and her feet feel heavier as she prays another teacher will reprimand the students before she can witness the scene.

"I really don't need this today." Thela bemoans under her breath, feeling her shoulders tense and ache as the clangor intensifies. "Why can't we all just coast into the weekend? It's like these kids have no sense." Then, the commotion abruptly dies, and it appears her initial prayers may have been answered.

If she had allowed her joy at the new silence to be seen, the shine of her gleeful, tooth-filled display would have blinded all that bore witness with the resplendence of a field of freshly fallen snow.

Oh, thank God! The educator mentally celebrates as she finally rounds the corner, revealing what seemed to be the culprits of the morning disturbance – a row of ten male students, members of the basketball team if their blue and silver jackets were any clue, standing side by side with their heads pointed at their feet as they avoid eye contact with their castigator: Silvia Lucero.

Silvia Lucero is the Assistant Head of School and The Pastor's assistant at Armonia Church. Though among the students, she is known as the glacial-hearted personification of the school's harpy eagle mascot: Steel Quill; uncanny in her ability to swoop in just in time to stomp out a student's mischief and unbending when it came to the rules of conduct. Her obsidian eyes pierce all that look into them like talons. This, coupled with her emotionless face and her stern yet gentle voice, lends her a natural authority that is acknowledged by all, including fellow staff.

If only they knew how lucky they had it. Thela chuckles to herself as she stops about twenty feet away to stand against the lockers and watch the scene.

Thela knows well that, despite her reputation among the students, Ms. Lucero's lectures are just stern talking-tos and nothing more; the most lenient yet effective punishment in the school. Ms. Lucero never angers. She never raises her voice, let alone yells. She never even punishes them; not a single write-up for a student's misconduct bears her name. *She's like an angel, her presence and words are enough to put anyone back on the straight and narrow.* Thela asserts with an amused grin as she watches Ms. Lucero wrap up her lecture and shoo the boys off to class. *At least for a few days.*

As the once rowdy basketball team walks away, Ms. Lucero rubs the back of her head, ruffling her short ponytail. *Such beautiful hair. I've never seen hair so dark and lustrous before.* Thela notes. *If mine looked like that, I'd never keep it short and tucked away.* Thela pats her short afro filled with damaged strands and split ends. *I sure wish I had the time to take care of this old puff.* She yearns.

In the middle of Thela's pining, Ms. Lucero notices the exhausted educator out of the corner of her eye. With a forced smile, Ms. Lucero waves. Thela, embarrassed by her staring, awkwardly returns the gesture.

"I wonder if she enjoys working here after so many years?" Thela mutters to herself. "I can't read her at all." Suddenly, the vibration of her phone interrupts her whispered ponderings, and the World History teacher quickly reaches into the pocket of her jacket. Her hands shake and her fingers tremble nervously as she answers the call, seeing the name "Jessica RN" flash on her screen.

"Hello?" Thela squeaks out, her voice cracking as she anticipates the reason for the call. "Is everything okay, Jessica?"

"Hi Ms. Hughes, sorry to call you at work, but it's about your father." The woman on the line responds warmly. Thela holds her breath, knowing what was to come.

"Hada!" A man's voice cries, drowning out Jessica's own. The voice sends Thela's mind into a frenzy.

"Yes, yes. I'm on the phone with her now." Jessica states, attempting to calm her patient down. "As I was saying, your father perked up all of a sudden after you left, and he won't stop yelling for you. Would you be able to...?" Jessica's voice becomes muddled nothingness as a cascade of emotions threaten to drown Thela.

"He's talking? He's awake?" Thela questions. The thought reverberates and intensifies within her skull; as if she was standing inside a ringing church bell, the notion blares so loudly she can feel the veins in her head pulsate.

Thela shakes nervously, barely managing to whisper out, "I'm coming."

Thela feels puzzled by the surge of emotions rampaging through her. *Maybe this is the emotional rollercoaster laboring mothers experience?* She jokes with herself–a failed effort to regain control of her ship plagued by the storms of relief, joy, pain, and sadness. But adrenaline fills her veins and pumps through her being still, and Thela can only stare at her hands as they tremble while struggling to return her phone into her pocket.

"Good morning, Ms. Hughes. Is everything okay?" a familiar yet cold voice asks, giving its best attempt at a warm tone. A lone match in the arctic, tasked with lighting a life-saving flame. "Thela?" Ms. Lucero's voice rings, finally breaking through the trance.

Thela, still staring at her quaking hand, can only stutter out a single phrase before dashing off toward her car: "I have to go."

With her blinders up, her surroundings become nothing more than white noise and blurs. The irony isn't lost on her, but not once does she consider slowing her pace. She blitzes through the halls and out the front doors of the school, quickly veering to the right once she is outside and the two heavy slabs of glass and metal slam behind her.

Her breath grows heavy and the muscles in her legs burn as she reaches the staff parking lot, her brick-red sedan peeking into view. *I haven't run like this since I was in high school.* she thinks, remembering her youthful days at this very school as she hops into her reliable, decade-old buggy. She throws her lanyard onto the passenger seat and starts the engine. She peels off toward the main road, the parking lot a mere speck in her rearview mirror.

With that, the frenzied storm leads to a flood. A flood of memories so vivid, so clear, that Thela feels as if a box of family photos is being dropped on her head.

Thela's nanny, waving to her from the porch with a joyous smile, as Thela waves back with her new "wand" she had found under the jacaranda in the front yard.

Thela's mother, sick and bedridden, patting Thela's head as she shows off a worm she had found under the same jacaranda.

Her childhood bedroom being struck with streaks of light poking through the curtains as her father pulls into the driveway after Thela's bedtime had long passed.

The shadowy figure of her dad telling Thela goodnight, as she pretends to sleep. Thela can still hear the faint "I love you." that always accompanied its appearance.

Young Thela, standing at her nanny's side as she feels the young woman's grip tighten around her tiny hands.

The day Thela realized her father was too sickly to ever go back to work. He's lying in the very bed her mother had withered away in and greets her with a weak, but warm, smile.

Her dad stands solemnly above her mother's grave in the distance as his shoulders tremble, hinting at the silent tears pouring down his cheeks.

Thela's grip on the steering wheel tightens, as she questions the string of misfortunes that plagued her family. "Are we just cursed?" She ponders aloud as she turns into her father's neighborhood, too deep in her own thoughts to bother with signals or stop signs.

Then, a lone figure peaks through the fog of memories, and Thela's eyes dilate with fear as she notices a person frozen in her car's path.

Thela instinctively swerves onto the sidewalk, narrowly avoiding the young man in the street. She thrusts her foot onto the brake, praying not to be claimed by the all-but-confirmed hex. Thela closes her eyes as her vehicle approaches a lamp post, expecting the worst, but the screech of her tires ends in dead silence. No sound of a crash; no impact felt. Thela opens her eyes to see the lamppost inches away from the hood of her car.

She takes a deep breath and jumps out, running over to the shaking, raggedy young man who had fallen to the ground.

"Are you okay?" Thela questions as she rushes to the boy's side and places her hands on his left shoulder. "I'm so sorry." Thela adds, trying to look past the jungle of ratty, blonde dreads that covered the majority of the young man's head and face. *He must be homeless.* Thela thinks as a knot grows in her throat. *But he's so young. He looks like he could be a senior at Armonia.*

Looking away from her, the dreaded boy nods yes, and accepts her hand as she gestures to help him up. Back on his feet, the young man stammers "It..it's, it's okay. I shouldn't have been standing in the road like that." The young man's chin shakes with every word, and he flutters his index and middle fingers wildly as he speaks. "I was just stuck in my own head. Sor..sorry for the trouble." The youthful vagrant turns quickly and dusts off his scabby knees that were visible through the holes in his worn jeans, ready to head off to God-only-knows-where.

Before he can jet off, Thela quickly grabs him by the arm of his oversized, navy-blue windbreaker and yells "Wait just one second." She pulls him all the way to her car, letting go only so she can reach in through the door and grab her lunchbox and lanyard.

"Here, take this." Thela commands, forcing into the youth's pockets all of the cash she had in the wallet attached to the lanyard, and handing him the lunch she would have eaten later that day before he can even register what she had put in there.

"Now what's your name, young man?" Thela asks as he looks down at the small lunch in his palms.

"It's...It's Will."

"Okay. Well take care of yourself, Will? It's only $40 and a turkey sandwich, but I hope it helps a little."

The young man stands in silence, raising the sandwich like a sacred golden treasure to his face as a smile takes over. "Thank you!" he shouts with joy, before tensing up and shrinking down like a child being reprimanded. He clenches his teeth and then, without another word, he turns and runs away.

"Also, Will, you should stop by the Armonia Church sometime!" Thela yells at the top of her lungs. "Look for Ms. Lucero, okay! She helps a lot of people like yourself!"

By the time she finishes her sentence, the mystery teenager is gone, and she can only hope that he heard her. Thela stands in place for a moment and stares at the corner where he disappeared.

Oh shit, Dad. She remembers before turning and jumping back into her car.

Once back on the street, Thela can't help but laugh at herself. *Take care of yourself? That's rich.* She muses. *What a hypocrite.*

Thela's eyes appear jaded as she looks along the winding road she has been traveling every day since her father grew ill. The neighborhood had become her cage; she never traveled more than half a mile away from her father's home. Not for work, not for groceries, not for errands. Even her own apartment, which she is only able to visit for brief but blissful moments between getting off work and Jessica's shift ending, is in a complex just on the other side of the main road. Her father had declined staying in a hospital, so all his care comes from Thela and Jessica the home nurse. But unlike Jessica, Thela always has to be on; she never has the opportunity to go out, decompress, or unwind. All just in case something happens.

As she pulls up to the off-white, single-story home and backs up into the driveway, Thela notes the dark bags around her chestnut eyes. "What is it? five years now?" Thela calculates under her breath before looking away and exiting the car.

Walking towards the door along the cracked, cement path ravaged by rising weeds, Thela looks out into the wild, patchy lawn that her father once took pride in. The once lush, amethyst jacaranda, under which she spent most of her childhood days playing, stands naked and tall, like a sentry guarding a once prosperous nation, now stripped of his ordain armor, yet not relieved of his duties.

"Hada! Time for lunch! ¿Qué tienes ahora?" A serene woman's voice calls from the cracked-open window next to the front door, but when Thela turns to answer the nostalgic cry, all she sees is the silhouette of her father against the curtain.

"Where is Hada?" She hears his husky voice question. "You really called her, right?"

Thela shuffles up to the porch and opens the door hesitantly. She notices Jessica seated on the bench near the door, but Thela's gaze immediately turns to the entryway that leads to the den that had been repurposed as her father's bedroom. His ceaseless grumbles at what must have been Jessica's refusal to call Thela roll into the hall like the clouds of summer drizzle.

"Thank God you're here. He hasn't stopped asking for you since I called." Jessica reports in a whisper. "Despite his numbers taking a turn for the worse this morning, he sprung to life right after you left for work. The sudden spike in energy has me a bit worried, but he won't let me check his vitals or give him his medication before you both speak."

Thela closes her eyes and purses her lips. "Why didn't you just help him? He can't stop you."

"Not how it works mam. He's of sound mind, I can't do anything he doesn't want. So, I need you to help calm him down so I can work." Jessica proclaims nonchalantly.

"Is that Hada you're talking to out there? Hada, come here!" Thela hears her dad's voice blare from the makeshift bedroom as the springs creak under the shift of his weight and the stretch of blanket at his feet tenses from his pull.

Well, here we go. Thela thinks, before pressing forward and swerving around the corner, entering the room. "Hi, Dad." Thela greets, smiling with all the joy she can force through her ever-constant exhaustion.

No matter how many times she had seen it before, the state of the man before her always shocks her. He who was once the strongest and hardest working man she knew, had become scrawny and sickly. His cheeks, sunken valleys between his jaws. His arms and legs dry, brittle blades of grass. His dark brown hair streaked with dusty-gray strands. *Is this where I'm headed?* She wonders.

"Hada you're finally here!" Her father cries with glee. "What was that Jessica whispering in the hall? She should have just sent you..." Her dad hesitates for a moment. "Are you okay, Hada?"

Thela perks up quickly and looks toward the window, realizing she had been staring. "Yes dad, I'm fine." She stammers.

With a hesitant glance back, she sees her dad point at the burnt-umber irises of his own, signaling her to say it again. "Hada…"

Once more, Thela lies to his face. "I'm okay, Dad."

JACOB HUGHES

"Well, you sure don't look like it." Jacob declares. "You look like you just got back from working in the fields. Someone your age should be full of energy like me!" Jacob raises his right arm and flexes his atrophied muscles, weakly patting his bicep with his left hand that is riddled with aged IV scars. "But it's probably my fault. All this energy is thanks to you doing all you can for me."

Hada simply looks away and shrugs her shoulders. "Don't worry about it, Dad."

Alright Jake, this is the moment you've been waiting for. What you've been preparing for during every moment you were too weak to speak your mind. Jacob thinks as he gathers his courage. "Do you remember why we call you Hada?" he finally questions after a long silence.

Turning her attention to the family photo on Jacob's nightstand, standing tall amidst a sea of orange pill bottles, Hada asks, "What's that have to do with anything, Dad?"

"Just humor your father. I haven't been able to speak to you like this in months." Jacob pleads.

Hada sighs and walks over to the thin, emerald curtains and pulls them apart, letting in the full glory of the early March sunshine. As she looks outward at her old, woody friend, and fully opens the window. "It had something to do with my old nanny, right?" She answers questioningly.

Jacob chuckles in response. "It has more to do with you and that jacaranda, but yes. Tatiana coined it." He sees Hada's shoulders shutter at the very mention of her former nanny's name, and then looks over to the framed picture on his nightstand. In the photo, he is seated to the left of his wife, who is laying on the bed with her back resting against the headboard, weathered by sickness yet still the same glowing beauty he had married. He holds her hand while in turn, a young Mexican girl with chestnut hair and terracotta-brown skin can be seen standing near the foot of the bed and carrying the then five-year-old Hada on her back. The girl was grinning proudly at Hada, who was raising a small jacaranda branch in triumph over her shoulder.

"You were always so full of energy and wonder. You spent all your time under that tree, looking for bugs, playing in the grass, and searching for branches." Jacob pauses and shakes his head with laughter. "Oh God help us if you found a branch. You'd just spin and spin until you fell from dizziness. Then you'd get up and show everyone your new 'wand'. Never putting it down, not even during dinner, until any flowers on it had fallen off. Then off you were to find a new one." Jacob can feel his eyes start to water at the cherished memory. "You were just so magical."

"Even when your mother got sick, and I had to hire Tatiana to help take care of you both during the day, that magic didn't leave you. The first time I brought her over, the first thing you did was drag her with you under the tree so she could have a wand of her own. Then, after your usual celebratory spin, Tatiana called you the cutest fairy in Chula Vista." Staring at the photo, Jacob repeats the phrase that gave Hada her name. "El hada más linda de Chula Vista. After that, the name just stuck."

"But when I look at you today, I can tell. Somewhere along the line you were forced to shut away that magic. All because you had to take care of your father and his weak body."

Hada's grip tightens around the open window frame as she continues to peer at the jacaranda. "Dad, don't talk like that..."

"This body would drive anyone to hate their life. Leave anyone begging to have it snuffed out. Watching yourself deteriorate to the point where even speaking is difficult, knowing you will never recover. It's disgusting." Jacob's hands tighten around the baby-blue blanket covering his legs and the man looks down at his useless limbs. "But it's thanks to this body that I can die happily."

Out of the corner of his eye, Jacob sees Hada suddenly relinquish the window frame and turn to look at her father. "Dad, stop talking like that!"

Still looking down at his legs, Jacob continues. "Once I was too weak to go back to work or live on my own, you came running to take care of me. Since then, you've always been there. I've spent more time with you these past five years, than I ever did when you were a child. I can't express how much I have cherished each and every moment" Jacob takes a gulp of courage. "But it's also because of this time, that I noticed you had changed. A change far worse than the one I saw after Tatiana disappeared. I began to think, maybe it wasn't just me, but my Hada that was trapped by this bag of bones. So, I hope with my passing, my joyous Hada will be free to fly once more, knowing her duty is done."

Jacob looks up to his mortified daughter and says plainly into her dark-brown eyes, "Thank you Hada, I love you."

THELA HUGHES

"Dad, don't talk like that!" Thela shouts as her father's tranquil expression leaves her insides churning. She feels sick. Yes, she is exhausted, but she never once wished for her father's death. Despite the circumstances, she too appreciates the time she has spent with her father. She loves him, and understands his past absence wasn't neglect, but an unrelenting quest to give his daughter everything he felt she deserved.

Jacob looks over to a photo that is hanging on the wall to his right; a photo of his Hada graduating high school, her smile beaming but her eyes dead as she is surrounded by friends and adorned with her azure cap and gown, paired with a silver and blue- knotted, honors cord. "When was the last time you went dancing? When was the last time you went out and enjoyed your life? It's been years since I heard you mention a single friend, and even when your coworkers invite you out, you always say no.

Her father then turns his attention to his palms, and stares at his trembling, boney fingers. "I don't want you to end up like I almost did, Hada. On your deathbed and all your memories are of work and struggle. If it weren't for your kindness and my body slowly being eaten away...If I were to have gotten hit by a truck or crushed by a beam when I worked construction, I would have died just like that."

"Do you regret it then? Working so hard for me and Mom?" Thela spits out. *What are you trying to say, Dad?* Thela screams in her head as she awaits an answer. Her father, momentarily shaken by the outburst full of desperation and pain, turns toward the family photo to his left and continues to speak.

"I would throw myself into the grinder a thousand times without regret if it meant taking care of you and your mother. My only regret is teaching you to live that way, and then putting you in a position where you have no other choice but to put the lesson to practice at such a young age." Her father declares, gripping the blanket with his weakening might. "You should be out there living and not just getting by. Dating, partying, brunch with friends, it doesn't matter. You should be enjoying life, even if it's only every once in a while. Even your mother and I were having fun at your age, I'm just sorry you never got to see that."

Time slows down to a crawl for Thela, and her heart feels squeezed by the sadness in her father's voice. *Say something, Thela. Anything.* Her conscious pleads. "Dad, I had plenty of fun before you got sick, and all thanks to you." Thela says with a loving smile, looking at her father's forehead as he continues to stare downward. "So, of course I have to return the favor. Besides, you always say I look just like Mom, so you should be happy that I got my character from you." She adds with a jovial tone.

Jacob grins and lets out a booming laugh that shakes his paper-thin frame. "Well, you are right about that. Good to know you've got some of me in you." Jacobs chortles.

There he is, that's my dad. Thela celebrates mentally. The laugh brings her back to long-gone dinners with her mom and dad. It floods her with memories of her and Tatiana staying up late to surprise and welcome her father home after a long day's work.

Jacob, still chuckling, looks over once more to the photo on his nightstand. "But I can't take all the credit. That Tatiana worked so hard she practically became your second mother. That's why I kept her around even after you started high school; I couldn't bear to tear you two apart."

That name, like a vine covered with poisonous thorns, constricts and pierces Thela's heart. "Well, that worked out perfectly, until she decided to abandon us my senior year." She sarcastically quips.

"Hada, hold your tongue!" her father suddenly snaps. Thela instinctively bites her bottom lip and looks down. "I can't believe you still listen to those cops' nonsense. Tatiana loved you as if you were her own daughter. She never would have abandoned you. I don't care if her purse was gone and there was no sign of a struggle. Those lazy pigs just didn't want to put in the work for a lowly nanny. I may not know what, but something terrible happened to that poor woman."

Thela remembers the day Tatiana began living with them after her mom had passed. She remembers Tatiana dropping her off and picking her up during her early years at Armonia. She remembers the walks back home and stopping by the corner store so Tatiana could buy her ice cream after she had done well on a test. She remembers how Tatiana cared for her when she had a cold. She remembers Tatiana sitting in the hall and waiting for her to return after going out to the movies with friends as a teenager. But most importantly, she can't remember a single time Tatiana had ever treated her as less than her own daughter.

*Oh Tati...*The fairy feels her heart wretch under the pressures of the thorny vines.

"I know Dad, you're right." Thela begrudgingly concedes as she stares at the worn wooden floors. "I just...I just wish I knew what really happened." Tears well up in the caged fairy's eyes as her heart struggles against the thorny vines. "What could have happened and why to her? Why her?"

"Would that make it hurt any less?" Her father questions. "Would knowing what took her from you, and why, make it any easier on you?" He finishes.

As the tears flow toward the floor, and its droplets splash onto her shoes, Thela whimpers. "No."

"I know it's hard, but all you can do is keep her memory alive and live the best you can, never forgetting how deeply she loved you. Knowing that she never abandoned you." Jacob proclaims. Thela sees her father's hand peek into view, reaching out for her. "And it should go without saying, but that goes for your mom and me too." He finishes with a chuckle as warm as a winter hug.

At that moment, the little fairy that felt abandoned by all her kin, looks her father in his dark chocolate eyes and grabs his hand. Struggling to keep her lower lip from quivering, Thela says, "Thank you for everything, I love you."

JACOB HUGHES

"I love you too, Hada." Jacob responds, following it up with a resplendent show of teeth as tears flow down his daughter's face. "So, promise me from now on you'll go out and live life to the fullest. Promise me that you'll be my free, little Hada once again?" The man begs.

His daughter just nods her head vigorously as she cries and leans in to hug her father. *She finally let it all go.* The man thinks. The relief brings with it exhaustion, and he can feel his will slipping. He can feel his body shutting down, and his mind becoming cloudy. Yet he never stops hugging his daughter as he closes his eyes. *I guess it's finally time to clock out.* The last image the man conjures up is the memory of his dear Hada spinning under the jacaranda when she was four years old. He cherishes the scene until his mind finally sinks into nothingness.

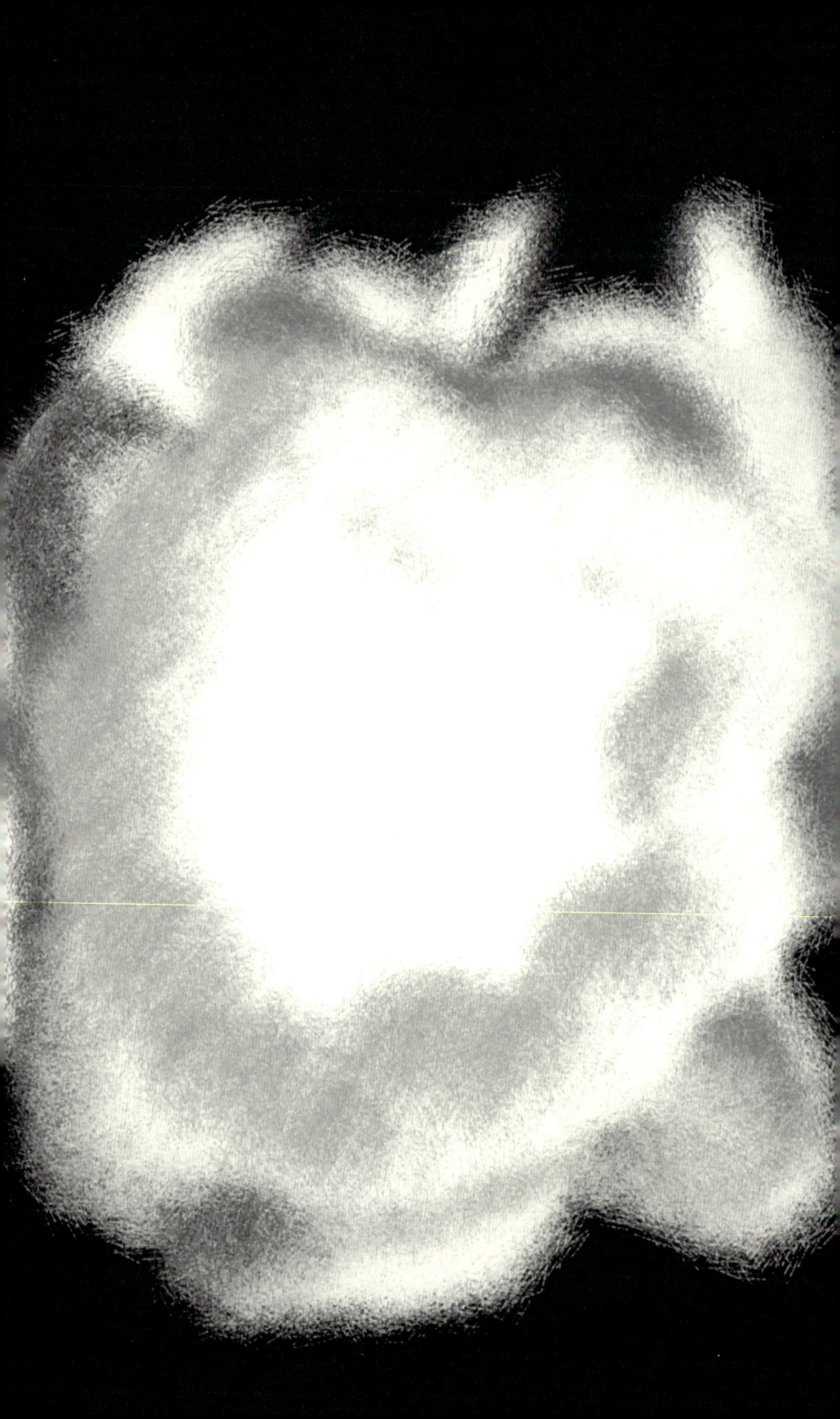

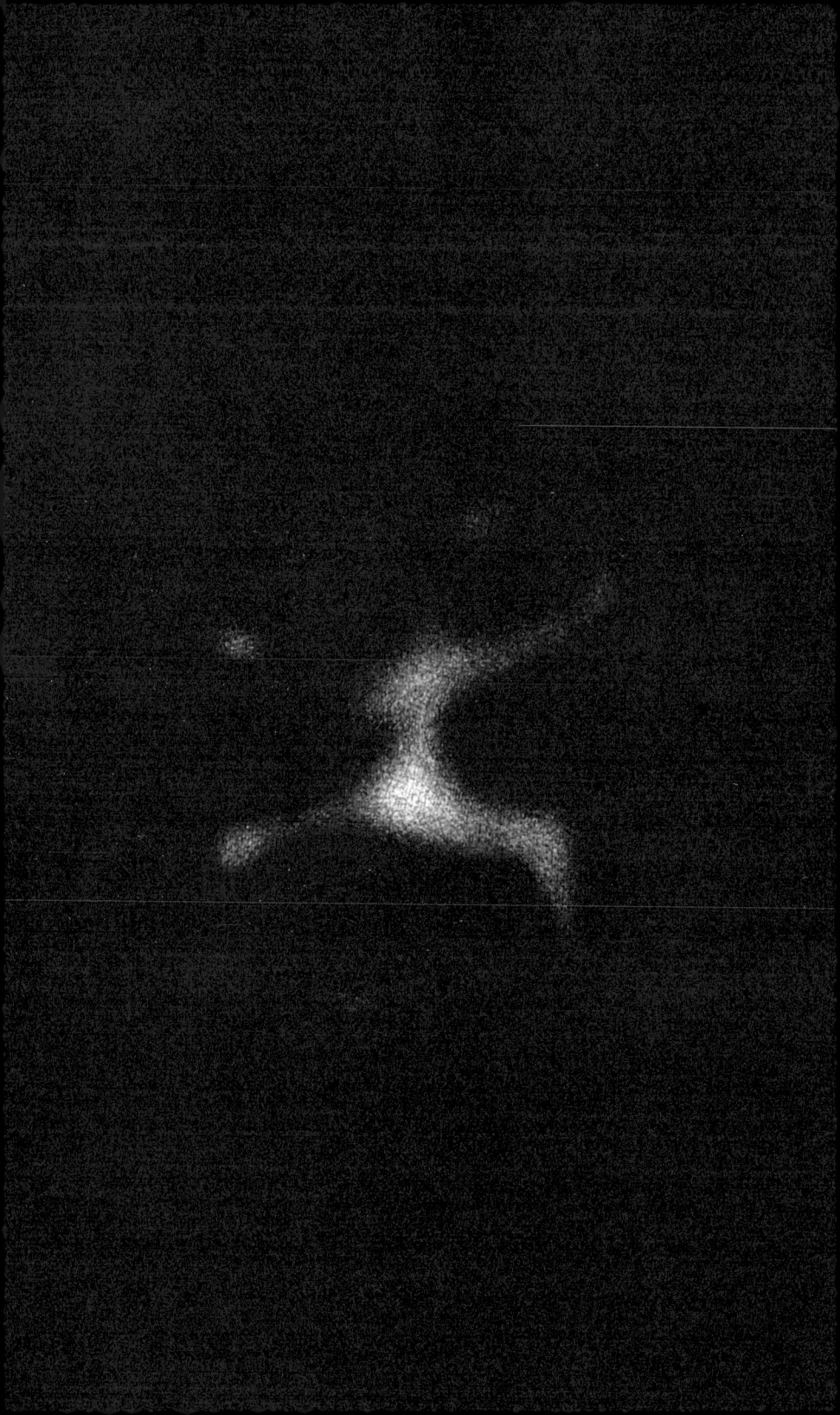

["Now."]

The eyes of the one known as Jacob slowly open up, and Thela can be seen sobbing on the shoulder of nurse Jessica.

["Now don't tell me all that crying is over my little nap. Pick your head up, Thela."] resonates Jacob's voice, drifting through the room with a new, alien timbre.

As Thela lifts her head slowly, Jacob's eyes meet her own.

THELA HUGHES

Perplexed, Thela wipes the streams from her face. She rubs her eyes, thinking maybe she was going crazy, but when she opens them again, there he is.

"Mr. Hughes!" Exclaims Jessica, as she rushes ahead of Thela and makes her way to Jacob's bedside. "H-how are you feeling?"

["I'm quite fine. Seems all the ruckus I was causing earlier really wore me out."] The man before her proclaims with a light chuckle.

"Mr. Hughes. You stopped breathing and your heart stopped pumping. I couldn't find the tiniest pulse and you were out for fifteen minutes." Jessica rattles off while scratching her head.

["Maybe you were too distracted by my daughters whimpering to concentrate. You probably just missed it"]

The man suggests as he pats her on the shoulder and motions to stand.

The formerly broken man jumps to his feet and turns toward his daughter with a smile. Thela simply stands in awe at the miracle before her. Her father, standing right before her very eyes. *Since when can he do that?* She wonders. *And his eyes. Have they always been so...black?*

["Well? Are you just going to stare at your old man like some sort of relic in a museum or are you going to give him a hug?"] Teased the man.

Shaking her head and ridding herself of any questions, Thela dashes over and hugs her father. "Maybe I wouldn't stare if you didn't sleep so deeply." She jokes with her father. Then she closes her eyes and hugs him as tight as she can. But something is off. She looks at his hair and notices not a single strand of gray is left. It was jet black. Even when she was a child it was never this dark. Yet, Thela continues to embrace her father, indifferent to a slight change in her father's hair color after God had given him back to her.

"Mr. Hughes, I'm glad you are feeling so lively, but I need you to sit down and let me check your vitals." Jessica pronounces as she taps both Thela and Jacob's shoulders. "You haven't been able to stand in months, so what if you collapse on the floor and hurt yourself?"

Thela can hear her father sigh as he concedes to his dedicated nurse. ["Jessica is right, Thela. How about while she tries to figure out what's going on with me, you go rest at your apartment so you can keep your promise and do something fun tonight. I assume they don't expect you back at work after the way you dashed out of there."] The man laughs.

"How do you know how I left work, Dad?" Thela questions with a laugh.

["I just know my daughter."] Her rejuvenated father replies with a sly grin. ["Anyway, it's time for you to let Jessica get to work. Remember, go and keep your promise. Take that new gleam in your eye and share it with the world."] The revitalized Jacob commands, turning his daughter and shooing her away toward the door. She looks back with a bit of concern but is welcomed only by her father's finger pointing toward the door, and his smiling face silently demanding that she leave. Thela looks over at Jessica's back as she sits her father down. ["I'm in good hands Thela, go."] Her father asserts.

With that, Thela concedes to her father with a nod and leaves him in the care of Jessica for the rest of the afternoon. She returns to her car in the driveway, sitting with a hefty thud. Nearly overwhelmed by the relief her father's condition brought, Thela shuts her eyes and takes in a deep, life affirming breath, praising God for granting her father more time on this earth; more time to make up for the lost years. With an enduring smile that pains her cheeks, she opens her eyes and starts the engine once more, driving straight to her apartment.

Once out of her father's neighborhood and faced with the intersection leading to the main road, Thela reconsiders sticking true to her promise. *I should call Ms. Lucero and explain myself.*

God, I hope she understands. Thela prays as she pulls out her phone and pulls up Ms. Lucero's number. The Pastor's raven-haired assistant picks up after the second ring, and Thela instinctively apologizes for running out of the school without a word before Ms. Lucero could so much as finish her greeting. Ms. Lucero's silent scrutiny seeps through the phone as Thela speaks, explaining the situation with her father in a rush and hoping that it will dull the harpy's talons.

As expected, Ms. Lucero is quick to verbally reprimand her and correct the behavior, but her criticism is quickly overshadowed by her gentle understanding. "You thought he was passing and you wished to be with him when he moved on. As a member of the church, I can't hold that against you." Ms. Lucero muses aloud in her naturally smooth, yet angelic tone; as if the subject was drawing her mind elsewhere. "Anyway, you've been through a lot this morning, so I doubt you'd be able to focus on your classes even if you came back today. Just head home, get some rest, and enjoy the extra bit of the weekend."

"Are you sure, Ms. Lucero?" Thela asks, though she had long ago turned in the direction of home in hopes of this exact proposal. *Please, please, please, please…say you found coverage.* Thela thinks, biting her bottom lip anxiously.

"I'm certain. I've been covering your classes since homeroom began. Everyone is so focused on completing their projects that are due next week that it's no trouble at all."

"Glad to hear it." Thela exclaims, surprised at the calm nature of the conversation. "Well, thank you so much, Ms. Lucero. I'll see you Monday?"

"See you Monday, Ms. Hughes. Now, go rest those legs, Speedy." Silvia replies.

Was that a joke? Thela wonders, never having heard the administrator jest before.

Their call ends as Thela parks her car outside her apartment complex, and Thela skips up the stair leading to her seldom visited, third floor apartment. The moment she steps inside, Thela locks the door, kicks off her shoes and throws her blue jacket onto the floor along with her lanyard as she slips to her room. Still feet away from her bed, she throws herself onto the mattress as the springs cry beneath the unexpected visitor's weight.

With her face buried in her pillow, and still wearing her tan skirt and white, collared shirt, Thela falls asleep without a worry to burden her dreams. A peaceful, healing darkness engulfs her, and she dreams of the day she met Tati for the first time.

When she awakes, feeling rested for the first time in years, she checks her phone and sees a message from Jessica stating that her father seems to be in great health. "It's as if he was never sick." She says before recommending Thela take him to the hospital the next day to get some testing done to confirm. "But just enjoy your night off, I'm certain your father will be fine without you for tonight."

Relieved further, Thela decides to go see a movie and puts on a modest, canary yellow dress she hadn't worn in years. *Maybe I'll get myself a drink at the movies while I'm at it.* She thinks, failing to remember the last time alcohol had touched her lips. Her tongue sings for the sweet company of appletinis. So, not willing to take risks on her first night out in years, she calls a cab.

After securing her chauffeur to and from her small night out, she gets dressed and heads out, rushing downstairs to meet the taxi.

"Hey there! Are you Thela? Hop on in!" The cab driver greets with an out of place, midwestern accent and a wave through the lowered, passenger-side window. Thela opens the tangerine-colored door and scoots into the backseat quickly, observing her cabbie from the back. He's a young-looking, chubby bear with a thick beard, wearing an orange shirt and blue jeans. His brown hair falls from under his baseball cap and down to his shoulders. "So just to the movies, huh? You don't see many people calling a taxi for a night out. I normally only get rich people going to the airport or old-fashioned dudes that hate using apps." The chatty driver says. "Yep, it's all about those ride-sharing apps now. There're even scooters all over the city that people ride around like tourists!"

"Well, it's been a while since I've gone out, and I trust taxis a bit more than a stranger's car." Thela states, slightly embarrassed. "Blame my dad for that one." She laughs, thinking back on her dismaying conversation with her father when he first learned about ridesharing while she was in college.

"Really? Glad to hear someone's out there keeping me employed" The driver jokes with a jolly laugh. "Now let's get you where you're going."

"Actually, before we head there, can we please swing through my father's neighborhood down the street? I want to make sure he's doing okay without me." Thela asks, showing the cabbie her phone with the address on the screen.

"Of course, Thela, no problem for me. Either way I get paid." The cabbie jests with a laugh akin to Old Saint Nick, grabbing the phone and entering the address into his GPS. "By the way, the name's Daniel."

Thela lets out a nasally laugh. "Nice to meet you Daniel. And you can call me Hada."

As a comfortable silence takes over the car, a radio DJ can be heard delivering quick snippets of news before the next song. "And speaking of tech, you won't want to miss this! *Davy-Swan*, the innovative robotics company whose creations range from surgical robots to drones, but that we all mainly know for their stylish, electric vehicles, will be unveiling their new model next month. They say it will revolutionize driving in all sectors, not just for..."

Daniel shuts off the radio with a huff. "Sounds like my friends may have been right. They swore they had seen a new self-driving car being tested around town, but I didn't believe them." He says, turning into Thela's old neighborhood.

I wonder if that has anything to do with that Abeona Rian comes to school in. Thela wonders. "I think I've heard about that too. But don't worry, they can't manufacture a personality quite yet, and you've got that in spades. You should be safe." She laughs.

Daniel's laughter joins hers as they wind through the roads, until suddenly the sky is lit with cobalt and scarlet. The cries of multiple sirens ring like a dirge; its source seeming to be in the direction of Thela's childhood home.

"No. No, no, no." Thela mumbles. Daniel, sensing there is a problem, asks her if that is the way they need to go. "Yes, please hurry!" Thela yells, gripping the headrest of the front passenger seat as she peers outward toward the road.

As they reach her father's street, Thela sees three police cars blocking entry. Despite her prayers, her childhood home that sat on the corner is indeed the source of the commotion. She feels her heart rip in two, seeing her father bloody and motionless on the grass. Just feet away from him is Will, the snake-haired young man from earlier, pressed to the ground and restrained by an officer. Blood is strewn across his face and clothes. Though the cop above him barely rocks back and forth, the boy's teeth, nearly clenched to the point of shattering, and the poison in his eyes betray the fight he is giving the officer.

Thela turns to Daniel in shock, hoping everything before her is a hallucination or some sort of dream. Daniel turns and looks back in disbelief as he stops the taxi. There is no need for him to speak, Thela can see it in his green-hazel eyes. It is no hallucination. Her father is dead, lying under the jacaranda.

DANIEL MILLER

Daniel watches as his first passenger of the night jumps out of the cab and runs toward the man on the grass. Before she can reach him, she is stopped by an officer who throws his arms around her, squeezing her tightly and keeping her just out of reach. "Dad!" She screams. "Daddy!" She cries again.

The midwestern cabbie steps out and stands next to his taxi, stunned and heaving at the tragic scene before him. The image of bloodied walls and a trashed living room enters his mind. A boy on the floor of the room lay silent with his eyes open wide; a trickle of blood falling from his lips.

Daniel's mouth fills with putrid salt, and he vomits as his knees give out and he falls forward. Narrowly saving his face from slamming against the unforgiving asphalt, Daniel's hands are scraped by the tiny pebbles of worn cement that riddled the road. The pain brings the cabbie back to reality, and he wipes his mouth with the back of his hand. Looking up, he now watches as the police officers drag the murderous vagabond into the back of the police car. Then, Daniel hears the young man yell out, just before the officer shuts the door.

"No, you have to understand!" The young man pleads.

"That thing is a monster. No human has eyes that black!"

PRISM 5

NO MORE

DANIEL MILLER

"Sir, we found another body inside the home!" A younger officer yells, running up to Daniel's taxi as he is being questioned by a detective. "It looks like a nurse that was taking care of Mr. Hughes. But..."

"But what?" The detective, whose name Daniel had forgotten as soon as he had heard it, spits out at the younger officer.

"But it doesn't match up with Mr. Hughes. Mr. Hughes was practically gutted, but this woman was sliced in the jugular and placed in the bed with care. That and the bag filled with Mr. Hughes' belongings we found next to the door..."

The detective raises a stern finger to silence the officer. "That's enough, kid. Let me finish with Daniel here, and I'll head in to check it out myself." He commands abruptly.

Daniel, who has only been half listening as he sits against the hood of his taxi, struggles to speak. "Ca...can I go now?" He stammers, staring at his wounded palms.

The detective's voice softens as he turns to Daniel. "I've got no more questions, so you're good to go. We've already got your information and Ms. Hughes confirmed your story, so there's no need for us to keep you here." Pausing for a moment, The Detective continues. "If I were you, I'd head home for the night. Get some sleep. No way you can drive around with a clear head after what you've seen.

Daniel balls his fists, interrupting the view of the scabs slowly forming on his palms, and turns to enter his car without a word. He collapses into the seat and slams the door shut, laying his head against the steering wheel. The familiar, cursed image of a bloodied living room, ransacked by a shadowy intruder and littered with broken glass, plagues his mind. Every attempt to forget only serves to make the memory stronger, until a feeling of defeat and grief takes over. Feeling his breathing speed up and panic seep out of his heart and into every limb, Daniel opens the glove compartment and reaches for an unlabeled bottle of off-white pills. The pills never take the horror of the memories away, they are no cure, but they help his body calm down when they make their presence known.

Daniel hesitates as his hand reaches the pills; this time, he can sense treatment won't be enough. *I need to see Finn.* Daniel decides. He throws the bottle onto the floor of the car, pulls away, and heads off to the only person that can help him clear his head and lift the weight off his chest; a weight he is sure will soon crush him otherwise.

Speeding out of Thela's neighborhood and toward the more affluent West Lake that Finn called home, Daniel struggles against the visions. It's as if despair itself has its scrawny, dead-purple fingers clenched tightly around his throat. He can feel its pin-like nails digging into his Adam's Apple as he struggles to breathe. *Please be home, Finn, please be home!* The distraught cabbie prays, swerving through the quiet, suburban streets of West Lake. While making the last turn necessary to reach Finn's street, his brother's past warning rings in his ears clearer than a cloudless sky:

"Now that we've got you settled, here's my new address. If you're in danger, come see me. But anything short of that, just call me. I don't know what I'd do if I lost you, too. Probably just curse the world and end it all. It's better for everyone if you stay away and live the normal life you always wanted." Finn advised with a loving firmness.

Daniel ignores the warning as he reaches Finn's two-story, sand-hued house, bringing the car to a jolting halt at the curb and jumping out of the vehicle. During a brief escape from the despair that choked him at the wheel, he notices a beat-up, gold sedan parked just across the street from Finn's driveway; an unruly weed among fine tulips.

That must belong to one of Finn's runners. Daniel assures himself, jetting up the short walkway and toward the front door. He knocks on the door frantically, as if despair had crawled out of the taxi and begun creeping toward him to claim him once more.

"Hey, hey, hey! What's wrong with you? I'm coming."

It's Finn! Daniel thinks, recognizing the unmistakable vexation that forever plagues his brother's voice.

A silence falls behind the door, as Daniel feels his brother's gaze from the peep hole, just before the rushed clicks and clangs of locks and chains sound from the other side. The door swings open and Finn stands before Daniel in the doorway, and a barrage of questions shoot from his perplexed, olive eyes. "Daniel? What are you doing here?"

JONATHAN FINN

"I thought you were my...why are you banging on my door? What's going on here? And did you leave your engine running?" The bewildered Finn asks, pointing at his brother's cab whose engine continues humming while it awaits the cabbie's return.

"That doesn't matter." Daniel spits out, seemingly eager to get to the matter at hand. He raises his hands in plea, revealing the punctures and small cuts on his palms.

"Daniel, what happened to your hands?" Finn questions abruptly.

"Finn, I need your help. I can't take it anymore. The nightmares, the stress, I just...I just can't anymore! Please, I'm begging you, help me forget." Daniel pleads, ignoring Finn's inquiry.

Finn, concerned, observes his younger brother, trembling before him. *He's never been this bad. What happened tonight?* Finn ponders with a tragic grimace. "I can't do that Daniel. You know better than anyone, what I have doesn't make you forget. And any joy it brings is a lie. It just makes you a slave. And I could never do that to you. Is the doctor still sending the pills as planned? If not I'll..."

Daniel drops to his knees and clenches Finn's legs, clinging to them for dear life and nearly kissing his worn sneakers. "Please, Finn, I can't take it! Death just keeps following me. The pills aren't working! I just want it all to end!" Daniel screams. "Just one see-"

"Help! Please!" Suddenly, his scream is drowned by another, and both brothers turn to see a girl, no older than eighteen, running from down the sidewalk with a mask of panic on her face. She notices them in turn, and sprints toward them; the blue and silver plaid skirt of her uniform billows behind her in a frenzy.

"Please, help me!" The youth yells with a labored breath. She trips just as she makes it onto Finn's driveway and falls with a loud thud and clink. She crawls desperately toward Finn's home, and Daniel scrambles to help her up and onto the porch.

What now? Finn wonders at the second disconcerting visitor, surveying his surroundings, and noticing the golden eyesore parked across the street. *Jacob?* Scads of potential scenarios play through his mind, but not a single one explains the situation unfolding before the skeptical, amateur chemist. Nothing added up, but life had taught him long ago that Daniel's mania, Jacob's empty car, and the hysterical girl wearing the Armonia uniform must have been connected. But keeping a low profile takes precedence over his suspicions.

"Get her inside, Daniel! I can't have all this attention on the house." Finn commands with a wave of his hand. Noticing a trickle of blood on her forehead as Daniel supports her into his home, Finn sighs. *Just what I need, a roughed-up teen with a black eye, bleeding and screaming in my yard in the middle of the night.* Looking at the girl's hand, draped around Daniel's neck for stability, Finn can't help but feel pity at the sight of her. Broken and bloody nails that sprouted from a hand littered with lacerations that, while not too serious, would certainly lead to a nasty kaleidoscope of scars. "There's a first aid kit under the sink. Take care of her wounds, I'll go take care of your car."

Mumbling expletives under his breath, Finn dashes to the cab, fiddles with the keys, and shuts off the engine.

"At least he was already next to the curb." Finn grunts out between a volley of curses. He snatches the keys and moves to jog back to his front door, looking back one last time at Jacob's vacant clunker. Then, after finally having a moment to slow down and play with the pieces, the puzzle comes together. *No.* Finn thinks as his eyes fling open at the epiphany. *No, no, no!* He speeds up, breaking into a full-on sprint as he tackles the door while turning the handle, rushing in to see his younger brother facedown and flat on the floor next to a simple gray couch, and the girl pointing a revolver at his head. Finn freezes and clenches his fist, as his heart rips in two. *No. Why today? Not Daniel!*

"Take care of her wounds." The girl mocks, while a small stream of blood continues flowing down her face; her thin, pink lips twisted into a defiant smile, like a lone salmon finally getting one over on the mighty grizzly. "I didn't expect such kind treatment from Jonny Appleseed himself."

Finn quickly collects himself and steps in further, closing the door behind him softly. "Daniel, are you okay?" He questions in a calm-yet-tense tone, looking at his captive brother. He only has one goal: de-escalate and get Daniel out of this alive.

"Tch...he won't be if you keep ignoring me!" The girl screams, bending down and pressing the barrel of the gun against the back of Daniel's head. "Now kneel, look me in the eyes, and beg me to let him go."

Ever the perceptive observer, Finn stares silently at the harpy's legs as her left foot digs into his brother's back, assessing his options. *Judging by those calves and thighs, she's pretty well*

built under that varsity jacket. Tall to boot. I don't think someone
as skinny as me can take her in a fight. Even injured. Not while she
has a gun.

The girl lifts her arm, drops to her knee, and slams the
butt of her revolver into the back of Daniel's head, knocking off
his hat. Daniel grunts but stays still as his assailant grabs a tuft of
hair and bends his neck back, forcing Finn to look into the oceans
of dread that were his brother's eyes. "I said kneel!" She screams
once more.

DANIEL MILLER

Daniel's neck shrieks as the vertebrae threaten to snap
from the forceful bend and his eyes clamp shut. Like a dull drill,
the pressure from the knee that had planted itself firmly
between his left shoulder blade and his spine intensifies with the
shift of his assailant's weight. And while Daniel can feel the
uncaring barrel tremble against his cheek, the screams from
every bone in his neck are too deafening for him to care. *Why is*
this happening again? Daniel whimpers within. *What the hell is*
wrong with me?

This pain isn't new, it is a sick nostalgia breathing new
life into memories from three years ago when the now-man was
only sixteen years old. Then, the pain came from a supposed
friend who revealed himself to work for a disgruntled associate

of their father, once a self-proclaimed, rising crime lord. Now a simple shadowy outline in his own memories, Daniel can only remember the paralyzing terror this trojan horse emitted once his true intentions poured out and the farce was complete.

"Where is the stash, Danny?" He hears as if it were yesterday. The Shadow asked the same question repeatedly. For every "I don't know", no matter how truthful, The Shadow pointed the gun to one of his five younger siblings, seated on the couch, and shot them in the head.

Tears erupt as the memoires play like a movie before his very eyes:

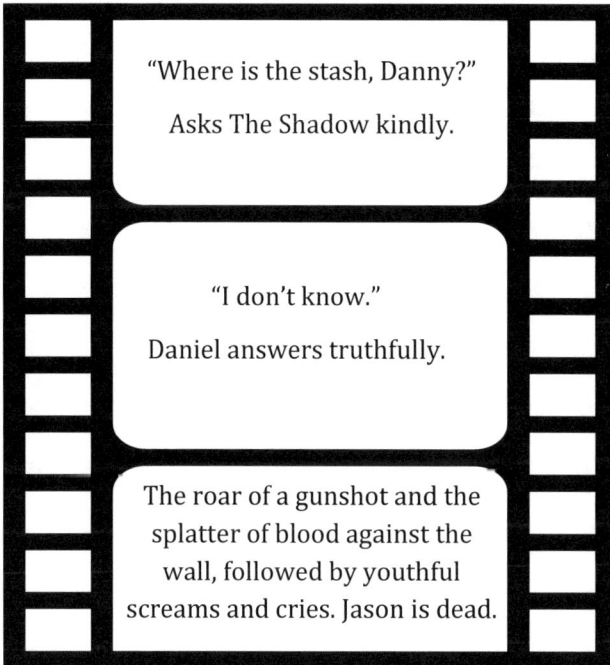

"Where is the stash, Danny?"
Asks The Shadow kindly.

"I don't know."
Daniel answers truthfully.

The roar of a gunshot and the splatter of blood against the wall, followed by youthful screams and cries. Jason is dead.

"So young, what a shame. Where is the stash, Danny?"
Repeats The Shadow, feigning sorrow.

"I don't know! Stop it!"
Daniel pleads desperately.

The thunder of the second gunshot is followed by a chilling silence. Lily.

"She was only seven, Danny. Why lie and steal her future?"
The Shadow pretends to ponder.

"I'll ask again. Please, just tell me the truth. Where is the stash, Danny?"
Asks The Shadow coldly.

"I told you; I don't know."
Daniel screams.

Another gunshot and more innocent blood added to the layers on the wall. Aaron.

"Where is the stash, Danny?" Asks The Shadow, clearly frustrated.

"I don't know, please stop!" Daniel begs.

Gunshot. Blood. Gerron. Whimpers from Terry, the last sibling alive on the couch, echo in the despair.

"Where. Is. The Stash. Danny?" Asks The Shadow, fuming with irritation. "You know what happens if I don't get a straight answer."

"Please, I'm being honest! Only Finn and Dad know where it is. We just do deliveries!" Daniel cries.

One last echo. One final coat of crimson on the wall. All that follows is Daniel's grief-filled scream, cursing his own existence.

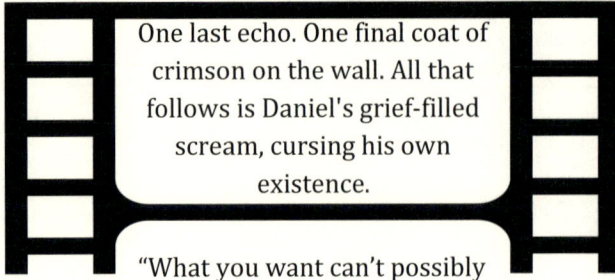

"What you want can't possibly be worth all this."

Finn asserts, echoing Daniel's final line in the tragic film and pulling him out of his trance. Daniel's eyes open to see his brother on all fours, with his forehead pressed against the floor as if he were praying.

"What would you know? I want you to beg for this guy's life like I begged your goon to leave my family alone!" The girl admits with a disgusted look. "Do you understand the lives you've destroyed? The pain you've caused?"

"Yes." Finn solemnly answers.

The grip on Daniel's hair loosens and his face crashes against the unforgiving, stone floor. Warmth and liquid build up in his nose, dribbling down his nostril and onto the ground.

"And... you just keep on pedaling your damned Eden Seeds? You care about money that much?" The girl questions, obviously taken aback by the honesty.

"It was never about money. And my reasons are my own. There are only two things you need to know. One: my brother only wanted to live a normal life and never supported me. Two:

killing either of us will only make things worse. So, just let him go, and let's talk." Finn's tense voice urges.

The girl sucks her teeth at the suggestion. "You sure are cocky for someone on all fours. What's going to happen if I decide to shoot you both? Are your goons going to hunt me down?"

"No, there are no goons. But all the same, the result I'm guessing you came up here to avoid would still play out if one of us died. Your best bet is to just leave." Finn suggests as he raises his head to look at Daniel's aggressor. "We don't even know who you are. You can just leave."

That lie, so venomous, stings Daniel's ears and brings them to a near boil. *He'd have her killed. He knows damn well where that uniform comes from.*

The girl guffaws and raises the gun from Daniels cheek. "I don't think so. I've done too much tonight. There's no going back now. So, let's test your little theory." The girl chimes as the hammer of the gun is clicked back. Daniel closes his eyes and prepares for it all to end. He prepares to finally apologize to Jason, Lily, Aaron, Gerron, and Terry.

"No, look! I'm begging you just like you asked. Please, don't do it." Finn cries out. "He's all I have left. Just kill me. Leave my brother alone."

"He's all you have?" The girl frigidly considers. "Good. Then you'll know exactly how it feels to lose someone thanks to your drugs."

It's okay Finn, just let me go. Save yourself. Daniel silently asks. Then, once again, Finn's warning rings loud in his ears, like the starting gong to the end of the world.

"I don't know what I'd do if I lost you, too.
Probably just curse the world and end it all."

Curse the world and end it all? Daniel ponders. Then Daniel, realizing what his death would mean, takes the deepest breath the girl's weight allows. *I can't let that happen.* Declares the cabbie, undoing the chains of survivor's guilt. *No one else can die, because of me.* Daniel abruptly pushes up against the girl's knee, throwing her off balance and onto the floor, perpendicular to himself. Quickly, she aims the gun at Finn, and glares back at Daniel.

"Not so fast, tubby." She warns.

Daniel, gulping painless breaths at the loss of the girl's crushing knee, manages to look her in the eyes and give his plea. "Don't do it! If anyone in this room dies, everyone taking Eden Seeds dies too." He yells with his right hand raised.

ALYSSA GARCIA

"What? Everyone?" Alyssa questions, her inner thoughts flying out of her lips. Even confused, the incessant pricks emanating from the cuts on the back of her hand remind her to never let her guard down. She stares back at Daniel as he slowly brings his hand back down to the ground, neither averting their gaze. Still, she sees that seed-pushing bastard out of the corner of her eye, grinning at Daniel's sudden maneuver.

"Yes. Everyone. And that goes for your family too." Daniel declares nodding to Alyssa as he studies her expression. "But no more. No one else is dying because of me, or my brother."

"Daniel, what are you saying?" Finn asks, appearing more confused than Alyssa herself.

"I'm saying we let her go, Finn. Really let her go." Daniel states, slowly adjusting himself to a seated position as he keeps one hand raised at Alyssa as a sign that he is no threat. "No more death, Finn. Let's end all of this."

I knew he didn't really plan on letting me go. Alyssa confirms, mentally patting herself on the back. *But Jonny seems upset, so this Daniel guy must not be following the script.*

"Let her go? No more death? End all this? Do you not hear yourself? I can't stop all this with no casualties. There's no difference between that, and this girl killing us both! None." Jonny spits at Daniel, his voice cracking from anger. The yell so jarring that Alyssa turns her attention to the seething dealer.

"Cool it!" Alyssa reprimands as she stands up, rushes over to Jonny, and points the gun at the side of his head. "I'm the one with a gun, so don't get any ideas now that your precious Daniel isn't eating the floor anymore."

Jonny starts to turn and look at Alyssa but is interrupted by Daniel.

"Calm down, Finn, we can figure that part out later. For now, just let the poor girl go. Please." Daniel requests once more.

"Let the poor girl go?" Alyssa laughs. "What do you think I had to do to get here? That I walked until God showed me the way? Idiot." Alyssa grunts between clenched teeth. "I had to kill. I had to steal. I'm no victim, and there is nothing waiting for me but a jail cell once this is all over." Alyssa digs the gun into the top of Finn's head, pushing his face downward. "So, stop acting like this snake gets to decide who lives and dies!"

"Well then hurry up and decide." Taunts Jonny. "Just know that if Daniel or I die, just like he said, anyone who has ever taken Eden Seeds will be right behind us."

That again? Alyssa thinks; the earnest calm in Daniel and the cocky tone, free of deceit, from Jonny concerns her. "Why would they be right behind you?" She finally asks, her voice shaken by her loss of control in the standoff.

"Because once you take your first seed, you need another. Once every five weeks." Daniel interjects solemnly. "Without it, the user dies from the withdrawal."

Alyssa's grip tightens around her gun. "And what exactly keeps them from going to the hospital like anyone else?" Alyssa questions incredulously.

"They can, but it won't do any good. This isn't your typical withdrawal." Finn states plainly, lifting three fingers above his head. "The Eden Seeds themselves are composed of three layers. An outer layer with a hallucinogen that provides the initial, intense high, a dense sugar layer, and an inner, solid pit made from a second drug. As the drug of the first layer is processed by the body and the initial high wanes, a byproduct is created that nestles itself in the spinal cord. This byproduct has the side effect of creating intense pain, so great that your heart wouldn't be able to take it. Think the opposite of an epidural." Reveals Jonny as he keeps his head down at the ground, now drawing an invisible diagram of his Eden Seeds with his fingers.

"Luckily, the sugar layer will have been eaten through at that point, and the second drug is released from the pit. This drug eventually makes its way to the spinal cord and interacts with the byproduct, creating a third drug that provides that nice sense of joy for three weeks, and inhibits the effects of the remaining byproduct. By design though, there is less of drug two than would be necessary to fully eliminate the byproduct, so by the end of those three weeks, the user starts to slowly feel the pain that will intensify until it kills them. Of course, when selling, we don't mention the whole pain thing, just the potential to die if the dose schedule isn't followed." Finn chuckles at the end of his story. "Most are so desperate and starving for happiness, the threat of death doesn't matter to them."

"What? Why would you make a drug that kills your users?" Questions the shocked Alyssa.

"Our stepfather used to say, there were only two things more powerful than addiction: Love and Fear. Given that love is unpredictable, he settled with controlling fear by using people's misery. That fear of death that comes only once people taste joy again will keep them coming back, even if one day their addiction doesn't, and they want to quit." Jonny informs. "That fear is more useful than money when it comes to controlling others."

Alyssa can sense the smile that creeped on his face as he revealed all to the ignorant heroine, her hands tremble at the glee in his voice. The meaning behind it bores through her like a parasite beneath her skin. *No. He's lying.* Alyssa panics.

"But to answer your question, I didn't create it and neither did our stepfather. That honor belongs to someone else. I'm just the last person on earth that knows how to make the precious seeds my thousands of users need to keep on living." Jonny states plainly.

With that, Alyssa realizes all her efforts were hopeless. Everything she had done that night - pointless, serving no purpose other than putting her family in the crosshairs of Jonny Appleseed. *I'm sorry, Daddy, I failed.* She thinks, as she allows her grip to loosen and her father's old revolver crashes to the ground in front of Jonny.

Jonny picks up the revolver and stands up slowly in front of the stunned Alyssa, who falls to her knees and hangs her head. *I was wondering why someone so important had no guards, why Jacob was so afraid to rat about his address. Only an idiot would threaten a man like him.* Alyssa grits her teeth, holding back tears.

"Good to see we understand each other now. Let's put an end to all this commotion." Jonny proclaims, stepping back with his left foot. Alyssa watches his right arm raise, aiming the gun at her head. "I've just got one question: how did you find my house? I doubt Jacob ratted on me. He was on Eden Seeds himself."

"He didn't give up your address, not even after four bullets in his legs. But, I was able to unlock his phone and this was just the address in his GPS app that stuck out since he wasn't exactly rich. Based on the history, he came here often, so I took a gamble. When I got here, I hid around the corner. I didn't have a plan, until I heard your brother's shouting." A dejected Alyssa admits.

Jonny sucks his teeth in annoyance. "Damn GPS. I'll have to watch out for that in the future." He says. "Well, that's all I needed to know. Try not to haunt me after this, I've already got too many ghosts."

Alyssa closes her eyes as one final tear runs down her cheek. *See you soon, Dad.*

Suddenly, Alyssa feels something slam into her, thrusting her onto the floor on her right. The thunder of the gun sounds, and a male scream quickly takes its place. Alyssa opens her eyes to see Daniel on the ground, gripping his shoulder as blood flows from between his fingers, body writhing in pain.

"Daniel!" Jonny screams, dropping the gun and running over to his brother. "What are you doing?"

"I told you, Finn, No one else. If she dies, I die." Daniel reiterates through pained gasps, staring deep into his brother's eyes.

Alyssa, too stunned to think, let alone speak, watches the two brothers.

"So, what do you expect me to do now? Just let her go? Let her get swooped away once she gets caught for killing Jacob so she can rat me out to try and get a better plea deal? Then what? We'd be in the same bind as we are now. Everyone on seeds dies." Jonny explains to his brother as he gently pries Daniel's hand from the wound to check how severe it is.

"Then, let's take her in. We can keep her safe until we can find a cure. That way, we'd have nothing to worry about."

"Take in the girl who just tried to kill us? Great idea." Jonny sarcastically replies.

"Y'know, she's a lot like you. Doing everything she can for her family, no matter the cost. Plus, you owe me one now." Daniel chuckles through the pain. "So, give her a chance."

Jonny sighs and sets Daniel's hand back over the wound. "It doesn't look too serious; I should be able to treat it here. Thank God you never went on that diet." he jokes with a forced laugh. "But, Daniel, there's no guarantee I can make or find a cure. I'm no real chemist; my knowledge of chemistry is limited to everything I learned while studying the seeds, so our chances of succeeding would be slim."

"Well then, I guess you better get studying again." Daniel pushes back, resolute as Finn helps him to sit up. The solemn admission had no effect.

Jonny pauses for a moment, and stares deeply into Daniel's forest-like eyes, searching. "So, you're really going to end your life, if anything happens to this random girl?"

"Yes." Daniel replies firmly. "I don't want anyone else to die because of us. That's why I decided to not give up. Why I decided to not let her kill me."

Jonny, still kneeling at his brother's side, hangs and shakes his head, chuckling at the audacity of his brother. "If only your idea were as simple as it sounds. Still, I'll take the slim chance, over the guarantee of losing you." Jonny turns to Alyssa, peering at her with his dull, olive eyes. "But, what about you? What do you think of his plan?"

"What?" Alyssa squeaks out of confusion, a grimace twisting her expression.

JONATHAN FINN

"What do you think of his plan? Do you want to work with us?" Finn repeats without blinking. "Beyond keeping you out of jail, it'll allow us to keep an eye on you, to make sure you don't get any funny ideas."

"As if you wouldn't turn on me at the first chance." Alyssa says, her face twisting in disgust, before softening with consideration. "But, let's say I believe you won't. What about my family?" Alyssa questions.

"What about your family?" Finn shoots back with an air of irritation.

"My mom. She's why I'm here. If what you say is true, she'll die in a week without another dose. Then my little brother would have no one."

Little brother, huh? Can't say I don't relate. Finn thinks.

"Well, of course, they can come with us too, right Finn?" Daniel asserts, assuredly nodding his head to the girl, causing Finn to turn and sigh at his brother.

"Assuming I have no choice, sure. I'll also keep producing the necessary Eden Seeds, so that all users can stave off their withdrawal until the 'cure' is complete." Finn plans on the spot. "Thinking about it, I will also need a current user to help me run tests once we get to that stage, so having your mom around will help anyway." Finn considers, looking up at his ceiling in thought. *But we're getting ahead of ourselves. We still have to cover up Jacob's death, and think of a reason for her family to move.* Finn thinks, looking back at Alyssa who is biting her right thumb and clearly struggling with the decision. While the bleeding had stopped on her hands and forehead, the cuts still needed to be cleaned.

"But let's think about this later. For now, we have to patch up Daniel, and clean and dress both of your wounds." Finn declares, standing and helping his brother to his feet as he stares back at the girl who finally releases her thumb from her dental hold.

"How do I know you won't just kill me and my family?" Alyssa asks as Finn walks over and stands above her. She looks up, and sees his left hand reaching out for hers.

"You don't. You'll just have to believe in Daniel and hope the slim chance works out." Finn slyly pronounces. "Now get up, we've got a lot of work to do tonight."

ALYSSA GARCIA

Alyssa, still cautious, takes Finn's hand with her own and allows herself to be jerked to her feet. Suddenly, she can feel the blood rush from her skull, and the lightheadedness that follows. The exhaustion and blood loss from the tumultuous night had taken its toll; the sudden rise was more than her body could take. Her vision goes black, and her mind goes still.

The next thing she knows, she's a little girl again, standing before her dad in a hospital bed. "Make sure you take care of your mom and brother. You know those two love getting into trouble. I'll be watching, the man declares with a laugh and smile. Te quiero mija."

Daddy, I did it! Alyssa thinks, screaming it as loud as her mind's lungs allowed. *Mom is going to be clean again!*

Yet, "Te quiero papa", was all that escaped from her lips, just as she had said years ago. Then, the room shakes, and the scene before her cracks, breaking into prisms that spin wildly around her. Their cold glow numbs her skin as they get closer with each rotation, and the pressure of their power suffocates her spirit. She falls to the floor, now riddled with thick scarlet blood, terrified but dazzled by the dancing shapes of the lights. Then, as the shivering lights near her flesh, the ground itself quakes and the sky rips open with a deafening roar. A line of flames cuts the sky in two and stains the surrounding clouds a fierce orange.

Just then, Alyssa comes to, realizing she is now awake and seated in a strange car. She can see her neighborhood, directly across the street from her school building, and in its center, just where her home would be, rises a tower of orange-tinged smoke. She starts to scream, but Alyssa's mouth is quickly covered from behind by a hand in black, fingerless gloves that clench her mouth shut. *Mom! Angel!* She mentally cries, seeing her childhood home be engulfed by flames.

"Your family isn't in the house, so please don't scream, Alyssa. It's been a stressful night." Finn's voice assures, calmly but stressed.

Alyssa looks out the corner of her eye to see Daniel in the driver seat, next to her. "Sorry about your house. Finn said it was for the best though." He says, giving an apologetic wave.

Finn loosens his grip around her mouth slowly, but Alyssa slaps it away before he can move it. Still, she keeps calm as she turns toward Finn's voice that emanated from the backseat of the car. "Then where are they? My family." Alyssa demands to know, her voice low but tense as she peers at the uncaring sunglasses of Finn. She can't help but notice his bummy attire from earlier had been exchanged for a nice pair of jeans, pure white tee, and a minimalistic, black leather jacket he wears over it. With his dirty-blonde hair combed back with gel, he almost looks handsome.

"Daniel and I called your mom, explained the situation, and told her to take your brother to the movies in exchange for free seeds. She was quick to believe and comply, considering Eden Seeds aren't exactly the most common street drug."

"Called my mom?" Alyssa questions aloud, confused at first, but quickly deducing the answer. "Did you use my fingerprint to unlock my phone while I was unconscious?" Alyssa asks rhetorically, looking at the embarrassed Daniel who turns away. *At least that explains how they knew my name and where to find my house.*

"Of course, I wasn't waiting for you to wake up." answers Finn, never looking up once from the game on his phone and tapping rapidly with his thumb at random intervals. "Anyway, before your family left, we had your mom 'accidentally' leave the garage open. Using that, I parked Jacob's car in the garage, making sure a neighbor saw me looking extra sketchy, before closing the door and secretly planting Jacob's body in your home, right by the stove, and turning on the gas. By the way, nice cliché. Placing him in his own trunk was convenient."

Alyssa rolls her eyes at the comment but listens without interrupting.

"After that, the final steps were just placing an unlit cigarette between Jacob's fingers, lighting a candle in the far room, and running like hell out the back and into Daniel's taxi. All that was left was to drive here and wait for the gas to reach the candle. Boom." Finn states calmly, allowing his left hand to reach for the codd-necked bottle of soda sitting in the back seat cup holder.

"You don't seem too torn up about framing and desecrating your friend." Alyssa questions, noticing Daniel's face twist with a tinge of regret.

"Please. He was simply my proxy and guilty of much worse than breaking and entering. Plus, it's not like I'm the one that shot him in the legs until he bled out." Finn asserts, as he pops the marble into the neck and takes rushed gulps of his Japanese soda. Alyssa feels her stomach churn at the memory of Jacob's blood pooling at her feet. The nausea nearly overpowers her as she tastes the salted remorse on her tongue. Alyssa quickly swallows the salty acid in her mouth, refusing to show regret in front of Finn.

"Hopefully, making it look like a break-in gone wrong will prevent an investigation into Jacob's murder. If it works, you and your family will be able to go on living without suspicion, and I'll be your cousin wanting to help out, welcoming you into my home while you all get back on your feet. That way I can continue to keep an eye on you, and make use of your mom when the time comes." Finn says as he finishes his drink and shakes the empty bottle in hopes of another drop falling to his lips. "Man, these bottles are so tiny, but I can't get enough of them." An electronic thud sounds from his phone. "Dammit! I died. Look what you did. Another life lost thanks to you." Finn teases pointedly.

"What did you just say?" Alyssa asks while balling her fist, her nausea instantly cured as she offers Finn the opportunity to change his comment; a poorly masqueraded threat.

"I said…" Finn starts, before being interrupted by Daniel.

"Guys, this isn't the time. We have to work together." Alyssa turns away and stares out her window. "It's either that, or you both end up losing the only family you have." Daniel reminds.

"What about the bullets?" Alyssa manages to say after a reluctant huff. "Can't they track those?"

"Thankfully, revolver casings stay in the cylinder. I removed all of the bullets in his legs too, so we are good to go there." Finn states with a sigh, placing his phone to the side and obviously disappointed by the tame response to his taunting. "The gun itself is still back at my place."

"Well, look at you guys." Alyssa compliments ironically. "When did you and Daniel come up with this plan?" Alyssa questions.

"'I'. When did 'I'?." Finn responds. "And sometime between you turning into deadweight and me patching up your wounds." Finn mocks. Alyssa looks at her bandaged hand and starts to feel a tightness around her forehead. Rubbing it, she realizes her head is wrapped as well.

I hope he doesn't expect me to thank him. Alyssa thinks. "So, what do we do in the meantime?" She asks. "I assume we didn't come all the way to my school to watch the fireworks."

"After you and Daniel forced me to change my ways, I thought this was a good opportunity to confess my sins to the priest." Finn dryly jests with a sarcastic chuckle while he reaches into his pocket.

"Here, put this hat on to cover your bandages." Finn states plainly, handing over a beany. "We're going to mix into the crowd from Armonia's Midnight Basketball Tournament. That explosion and the coming sirens are bound to draw everyone out.

Alyssa raises an eyebrow at the seemingly unnecessary step. "Why would we need to do that, if your plan supposedly moves all suspicion away from me?"

"Just in case any of my neighbors saw you after your stunt tonight in my driveway. Can't have them recognizing you from the news and asking questions without having an explanation." Finn points out. "We have to start playing that cousin angle now, claiming you came by my home with Daniel before the game and pranked me by pretending to be chased." Finn adds. "If anyone brings up that they recognized the car in your garage as the car parked across the street from my home earlier that night, we'll just claim that Jacob must have been stalking you and went to break into your home afterward."

"I see." Alyssa states while placing the hat on her head, making sure the bandages were completely covered.

"Yep, follow my plan and we'll be golden." Finn brags, looking out the window toward groups of students and parents leaving the school building through the gym doors.

Cocky bastard. "By the way, Armonia isn't catholic." Alyssa jeers.

"Huh?" Finn stammers, the door opening with a thud as he pulls the handle.

"Armonia isn't catholic. It's non-denominational. We have a pastor and no confessions. For all your planning, how'd you miss that?" Alyssa scoffs as she opens her own door and peers over her shoulder mockingly. "Also, what's up with the stupid shades? It's like 11:30 at night. Still trying to look super sketchy?"

Finn pauses, looks outside the car, then scowls and lowers his sunglasses in anger, looking Alyssa deep into her soul. The sirens of distant emergency vehicles speeding down the road to put out the flames of her former home fill the gap in the deathly silence. "You're lucky we have to seem like innocent, loving cousins right now. Now, get out the car, and act like someone whose house might have just blown up. The crowd is leaving the building."

JONATHAN FINN

I can't stand this girl. But, I have to keep it together for Daniel. Finn thinks, stepping out of the car and raising his sunglasses back up, now self-conscious about his fashion choice. *Maybe the sunglasses are a bit much.*

Hello there! A kindly, but concerned, voice cries toward Finn as he closes the door to the taxi. "Ahh, Alyssa, is that you? Who are your friends?" A tall, middle-aged man, dressed like a used car salesman, asks while strolling up to Alyssa, his pearl skin contrasted by the flush cheeks of a wide smile.

"Hi, Pastor Sawyer." Alyssa greets with a wave of her unwounded left hand, as she hides her right in her jacket pocket. "These are my cousins! Finn and Daniel. Finn, Daniel, this is the principal and founder of my school, Pastor Sawyer." Alyssa introduces with a warm tone, but a tense, warning glare.

Finn feels a nudge at his arm, and notices Daniel, his eyes pleading the older brother to greet the pastor back. "Hey there, Father." He says with a begrudging wave.

"Nice to meet you, Mr. Finn and Mr. Daniel. I wish your first visit to Armonia Church and School would have been on a less chaotic night." The pastor smiles back.

"I know how you feel, Pastor Sawyer. They just moved into town not too long ago, so I thought it'd be nice to take them to the big tournament. But as soon as we parked, there was a huge explosion in my neighborhood right there." She fibs, feigning concern.

"Oh, my goodness, well that explains the noise and the sirens. Have you called your mom to check if everyone is okay?" The pastor asks.

"I just got off the phone with her. She and my brother are still at the movies, thank God." Alyssa responds with a worried glance toward the rising clouds of black and orange. "She told me to stay here with my cousins until she calls again since there's no telling what just happened."

"That's certainly for the best. Actually, we just decided to clear the building and send everyone home after hearing the explosion and sirens. Just in case. Such a shame, the games were just getting started and everyone in town always looks forward to them." The pastor shakes his head in disappointment before continuing. "Well, nice to meet you, Finn and Daniel. Alyssa, you three are more than welcome to come with me and stay in the main church building until all of this commotion is over." The pastor offers. "If that is okay with you two, Mr. Finn and Mr. Daniel."

"Just Finn. You can just call me Finn. Thanks." Finn says as he crosses his arms, barely hiding his malice with a badly faked smile and thanking the stars he was wearing his sunglasses after all. *So, this is the guy?*

"Oh, we'd really appreciate it! Best to stay close in case our Auntie needs any help, right Finn?" Daniel chimes in, patting Finn on the back.

"Yeah, I think you're right." Finn answers, scratching his head and nodding awkwardly. "Thanks for your hospitality, Father."

"I'm no father" The pastor laughs. "Well, just follow me, you can all have a seat in my office behind the sanctuary."

"No father" my ass. Finn thinks as he gestures Alyssa forward, and all three follow the pastor to his office in the church.

PRISM 4

CLIMB OR SINK

JONATHAN FINN

As Finn trails behind the pastor and Alyssa, with Daniel at his side, he notices a large bird circling above the church. *Never seen a hawk or eagle flying at night before. Then again, what do I know about animals?* He thinks, scanning the church grounds, curious for what prey the bird sought. Beyond parents and students heading to their cars, which he deems a ridiculous hunt for the bird of prey, he sees no signs of life. Then, two thin scarlet beams pierce through the darkness from under the shadows of the roof of the church, just under a window on the ground floor and toward the back. Two eyes, giving off a demonic glow, stare back at Finn, causing his heart to skip a beat.

The sound of the sirens die and Finn's surroundings are all but erased as his mind fixates on the strange sight. As he stares, he can feel the creature's judgment; it's discerning, patient, and intelligent nature. He can only imagine the sharp toothed maw, ready to pounce at his throat, that the night allowed to remain hidden. It was death in waiting.

"You okay, Finn?" Finn hears as his body is shaken lightly by familiar hands. "You spaced out there for a second. What are you looking at?" Daniels asks, concerned.

Finn looks at his brother, confused. "Do you not see that..." In the time it had taken Finn to look at his brother and back again, whatever creature had been lying in the darkness had left; all that remains are the shadows. "Never mind. I think I was just seeing things. I thought I saw a weird dog or something under that window, but it's gone now."

"Wouldn't surprise me if you did." Interrupts the pastor. "Lots of strays find their way to our doors, people and animals alike. But Ms. Lucero takes care of them all."

The pastor's nonchalant tone calms Finn's concerns for a moment, despite the hawk still circling over Armonia Church. "In fact, if there is any issue with you returning home tonight, we can ask Ms. Lucero if we have room for you all to stay. Anytime I've seen or heard of explosions like that, especially in a residential neighborhood, it's always a gas leak. It may not be safe for you all to return home tonight."

"No need." Finn quickly replies, though still distracted as he watches the hawk wheel around the sky of the church. "If push comes to shove they can stay with Daniel and me. We have plenty of room in our house."

"I see, I see. Well, that's fantastic news; having family like yourselves in the area." The pastor responds with glee.

"Whoa…hey, look at that bird, mom!" Finn hears an excited, juvenile voice cry from the opposite end of the parking lot, toward the main road. "What do you think it is?"

"I don't know, a hawk?" A tender voice responds with a chuckle.

"Wrong! Hawks are diurnal. They're only awake during the day." The eccentric teen says playfully, imitating a game-show buzzer. "Try again!"

"A vulture?" The woman, who must have been his mother, responds questioningly.

"Wrong again, they're diurnal too." The know-it-all answers.

"Then, what is it?" The mother asks.

"I don't know. I'll try to figure it out tomorrow when Rian and I stop by the library for the first stop on his Birthday-City-Tour." The young man says with the curiosity and passion of a scientist on the brink of discovery. "Can you believe he's never been to the library or celebrated his birthday?"

"The birthday thing, no. But the library, I believe." The mom laughs, "You're the only one who still goes to the library for fun. Don't you want to take him somewhere more… festive?" She jokes.

Finn looks over to his left, at the talkative pair, as he finally passes them. The boy is wearing a lustrous, silvery hoodie that shines in the night, only outdone by his cheeky smile. Even when they stood across the parking lot from each other, that grin was clear as day, irritating Finn. *How great it must be to live so carefree. Even with all the commotion, he's more concerned about a bird than the pillar of smoke and sirens.* Finn thinks, turning his attention to the mother. In contrast to her son, the Indian woman's outfit is muted. A pale orange, knit sweater and worn, black sweatpants that seem better suited for a night at home than a social outing. She has the same rich, peru-brown skin and dark hair as her son, though hers lacks his thicker curls.

The youth, looking earnestly confused, raises an eyebrow. "More fun than the library? Nothing is more fun than West Chula Vista! Plus, I think Rian is more excited than I am. He only agreed to join me after I mentioned the new 3D printer in the lobby; they have it making one of those grippy hand toys. You should have seen those eyes shine when I brought it up."

"Well, speaking of strays." The pastor notes aloud. "I see you've dragged your poor mother along yet again, Nesho!" The pastor yells across the parking lot toward the mother-son duo, who wave back.

"Of course, you know this is our monthly tradition, Pastor Sawyer!" Nesho yells back warmly.

"Sorry that the game got canceled, Nesho. I know you both always look forward to it. How are you doing, Shazmin?" The pastor yells back.

"We are good! And don't apologize. Even Nesho knows it's better safe than sorry. We'll probably just head home and watch a movie." She yells, cupping her hands around her lips, before her eyes open wide as If she had forgotten to say something. "Oh, and don't forget, I'll be leaving for a business trip after I drop him off at the library tomorrow. Silvia is supposed to pick him up so he can stay with you all for the weekend."

Home? Finn wonders.

"Of course, we could never forget about our favorite troublemaker! One of us will pick him up! Now, enjoy the rest of your night! Stay safe!" The pastor yells one last time, before turning away and continuing to lead the three abettors through the main church door, and into the sanctuary.

"We will!" Finn hears the young man yell back as he turns to follow Pastor Sawyer. "And I hope you're ready for a good show tomorrow night. I've been practicing!"

The pastor simply chuckles, and waves back without turning to face the duo again.

"You called them strays, right?" Daniel asks Pastor Sawyer. "Wouldn't their home be here?"

The pastor hums for a second before responding. "Well, their situation is complicated to say the least. Shazmin found us when she was young, still pregnant with Nesho, and disowned by her family. Her boyfriend, Nesho's father, was still with her at the time, but his family didn't approve of the relationship nor the child, leaving Shazmin with nowhere to go. Desperate and having heard the rumors of our church's efforts, she came here seeking help from our resident saint, Silvia Lucero."

Well, doesn't that sound familiar. Finn bitterly reflects.

"With a secure home, she managed to finish high school, but finding a job during a recession with no college degree was quite the herculean task to say the least."

"Lucero? Is Silvia the same Ms. Lucero you mentioned earlier? Who is she exactly?" Daniel asks.

"Ms. Lucero is our vice principal at the school and the pastor's assistant at the church." Alyssa answers instead, breaking her silence.

"Well, yes, that just about sums it up. Officially, she's the Assistant Head of School and The Director of Operations at the church, though that is purely due to lack of financial backing and framed qualifications to hang on the wall. In my opinion, she should be running the whole of Armonia Church and School." The pastor chuckles. "She's the only reason I started to work at this church, and ultimately opened the school. She's the reason Armonia is what it is today."

"Really?" Alyssa questions incredulously. "She's so strict, stern, and serious. I can't imagine such a scary person inspiring you. You're so…"

"Warm. Kind. Affable." The pastor brags with a laugh, filling in the blanks. "I'm surprised, the heart of our soccer team and vice president of the new Judo Club is just like everyone else, when it comes to her. I was sure you were fearless." The pastor jokes at Alyssa's expense. She looks away, slightly embarrassed.

Alyssa pokes her index fingers together repeatedly, searching for the best way to describe her least favorite member of the staff. "Well, yeah. She can be a bit...I don't know."

Well, look at her. You'd think she was just any other high schooler, talking to her principal. You'd never guess she killed someone tonight. Finn laughs to himself. "What's wrong Alyssa, has she been mean to my poor little cousin." Finn jests, nudging Alyssa with his elbow. In turn Alyssa glares back, with a fierceness that nearly shatters his sunglasses. *There she is.* Finn thinks smugly.

The pastor chuckles with amusement. "Despite her tone and stern face, she's an angel. But just like the angels of the bible, the natural reaction to her overpowering aura and spirit shaking voice is always fear. Her obsidian hair and matching eyes that pierce your soul don't help either, so, just like those angels, it is through her actions alone that anyone can discover the tireless force for good that she is." He says, having taken on an educational tone.

Opening a door in the back of the sanctuary, Pastor Sawyer leads them into a thin, I-shaped corridor. Two bathroom doors stand to the right and left near the entryway, labeled "Men" and "Women" respectively. Further down the corridor are five evenly spaced doors on each side that lead to double doors at the end of the hall. "But, you better start whispering or, come Monday, the harpy may come for you." The pastor jokes, pointing to the first door on the right of the hall. "That's her room, right there."

Alyssa stiffens up, visibly fearing the consequences.

"I'm just kidding. She's still outside, vacating the gym and parking lot, and gathering our new 'strays' so she can show them their rooms. You're safe, for now." Teases the pastor. "But that brings me back to my favorite set of 'strays'." Pastor Sawyer remembers aloud, steering the conversation back to Nesho and Shazmin. "As I was saying, Shazmin came to us for help when she heard we had a few open rooms, and Ms. Lucero allowed her to stay here. Good thing too. That no-good, ex-boyfriend of hers eventually left the poor girl to fend for herself soon after Nesho was born."

"So, anyone that comes and asks can stay for free? Pretty sweet deal." Daniel proclaims.

"Well, not exactly," The pastor replies. "Ms. Lucero has a knack for reading a person's heart. If she doesn't approve, you're out. Just like that. It just so happened, Ms. Lucero saw not only good, but greatness in that poor girl. She ended up staying with us for nearly eight years. Up until she got out of law school and established herself." The pastor smiles as he stops in front of the door next to Ms. Lucero's room. "In fact, this room essentially belongs to Nesho. He still stays every now and again, usually when Shazmin has a work trip. He's spent so much time here, he says it still feels like home. The pastor shudders. "Even if he keeps me up at night with his borderline obsessive violin playing, I'm happy he thinks of this place so fondly."

"That's great for Nesho and his mom, but that doesn't seem a bit cruel to you?" Alyssa asks with a bewildered look. "Rejecting someone with nowhere else to go based on just one person's opinion, so easily?"

"Like I said, Ms. Lucero is never wrong. And our turn away rate is rather low; most people that wouldn't get her approval don't bother speaking with her very long. The moment they hear her ask how long they wish to stay, they leave in a panic." The pastor informs solemnly, unexpectedly serious, before turning around and flashing a smile toward the group.

"There was only one time I ever thought she might be wrong: when she told me that I was still capable of helping people and finding my own purpose. She said the fact that I didn't run with my tail between my legs at the sound of her voice, was proof enough." He turns back around with a nostalgic grin and continues toward the double doors at the end of the hall.

"If you didn't believe her, why did you stay?" Alyssa questions.

"Who knows." The pastor says, with a reflective chuckle. Maybe that's just another superpower her icy voice has. Maybe, even though I thought she was wrong, something deep down inside me wanted her to be right."

This response leaves Finn unsatisfied. "So, what kind of person were you then, before all this? What kind of person wouldn't believe there was any good left in them?" He asks.

"The kind of person who had lost his faith. After the wolf that raised him, shed its sheepskin." The pastor states bitterly, opening the door and revealing a tidy, uninteresting office, with a door to the back-right that revealed a bedroom with light furnishings. "Oh goodness. I must have forgotten to close my door, give me one second. You all can have a seat at my desk if you'd like." The pastor offers as he rushes to shut his bedroom door.

"Thanks, don't mind if we do. So, about that wolf. Who was he?" Finn asks, ensuring the topic at hand isn't lost.

The pastor looks at Finn, a befuddled look crosses his face as he takes a seat at the head of his desk, opposite his three guests. "Strange, I am very open about my past and use it as a source of inspiration in my sermons. I was certain it would be the first thing that students mentioned about me, but I guess I was wrong."

The pastor clears his throat, searching for where to begin. "The wolf was my father; a pastor like myself, in fact. Long story short, he raised me in the church, sent me to school for religious studies, and pushed me to become ordained. I looked up to the man. As any young man would have. And then, he showed me what it truly meant to run a financially successful church. Money laundering, lying, abuse, and more."

The pastor looks across all the faces seated before him. "After that, I lost heart. I lost faith. I dedicated myself to being a liability to my father's church, trying to ruin his good name by becoming the embodiment of his sins. I publicly engaged myself in all the sin I could stomach. Casual encounters with women, drugs, lying, stealing. You name it. If it isn't violent in nature, it's probably on the list." Pastor Sawyer begins to rub his forehead in frustration, but then continues. "Yet with his connections, it meant nothing. He was able to sweep everything I did under the rug, allowing me to fall deeper into sin so I could drown out my own self-hate and powerlessness. I became a wandering lush. My meal of choice was pills, and my drink was bad tequila." The pastor looks Finn directly in the eyes, a gaze that nearly pierces his sunglasses. "One of my benders landed me here, where I met Alyssa's father. He was the officer who was patrolling the area one night and saw me throwing bottles at the church doors. He was just about to arrest me until Ms. Lucero came out. She asked me why I was throwing bottles at the church. I told her it wasn't personal; I hated all churches. After that, she asked him to let me go. You know the rest."

"So what? You just started to work here and eventually became the charitable pastor of Armonia? You just let go of all that hate?" Finn questions, slightly annoyed at the briefness of the story.

"Hard to say. The newfound purpose and passion that my conversation with Ms. Lucero gave me eventually led to me using my hate for good. For my father's part, he was happy to fund my new goals, even if they were in another church. It was something he could brag about." The pastor chuckles warmly to himself. "Eventually, he was so happy about the growth of this church and the new school, he put me back in his will, and on the very day he died I not only acquired his wealth but was offered the position of head pastor at his church. Alongside Ms. Lucero I requested the former pastor of Armonia to take his work to my father's church in my stead, knowing they needed a new, proper leader. I was able to end the corruption of one church and raise another. I used what was once evil, to spread that much more good. Not only that, I also found my lord again, and it was all thanks to Ms. Lucero."

"You didn't answer my question." Finn points out. "Do you still hate your father?"

The pastor raises a brow at Finn, whose attention on the pastor's next words is palpable. He looks at the ceiling, and chuckles epiphanically. "I haven't really thought about it in years, but I do get a kick out of showing the old man up and replacing the corrupt, old guard that ran his church. Maybe that part of me does still harbor some ill feelings toward my old man." The pastor then looks down with a gentle-but-serious gaze. "Now, tell me why some night-shade-wearing, twenty-something, who should be worried about his cousin's home, is so concerned with my past."

Dammit. Is he on to me? Does he know who I am? What if he starts to suspect that we aren't cousins with Alyssa? Finn panics, sweat beading on his forehead. *I can't have our plan ruined by this bastard. If I can just force a seed down his throat, then...*

"Finn and I don't exactly have the best experience with dads." Daniel interjects, saving Finn from his own muteness. "We didn't know our real father, and our stepdad was into some shady stuff to say the least. He was pretty abusive to boot. Though our mother did her best, eventually his lifestyle dragged her down too and led to her being put away and him being put in a coffin. It was only three years ago when we lost everything, but Finn, at just nineteen years old, stepped up and took care of the both of us. He even dropped out of college so I'd be able to focus on my studies and finish high school." Daniel turns to Finn and nods his head. "His bad-dad story felt familiar to you too, right?"

Thank you Daniel. Finn thinks. "Yeah, it did. Sorry, Pastor Sawyer, I'm just a bit awkward." Finn stammers, lowering his head out of embarrassment. *I can't believe I'm apologizing to this guy.*

"No, no. You are perfectly fine. I'm sorry to hear about all of that. It must have been hard growing up in that environment."

"You make the best of what you have, right? Finn and I have always had each other, so that's all we need." Daniel slaps Finn's back out of comradery; the sting causes Finn to grimace and his sunglasses slip to the tip of his nose. "He's a bit rough around the edges and sometimes he can let his anger get the best of him, but we're working on that."

"Anger you say?" The pastor thinks aloud, clinging to the word as if he had found the answer to life itself. "So, Finn, your questions. Do they have anything to do with this anger?"

"No." Finn responds solemnly, pushing his glasses back up into place and looking back at the pastor. "And honestly, talking about all this is starting to piss me off. I appreciate you allowing us to wait here, but I think it's about time we got in contact with Aunt Holly so we can get out of your hair." Finn thrusts the chair back and rises to his feet. "Alyssa, try calling your mom. She should have heard something by now."

Alyssa looks perplexed at the sudden shift in mood. "But it's barely been fifteen minutes." She asserts, but her claim is met with neither words nor a gaze. "Fine." She concedes.

In the midst of his deathly stare down with the pastor, out of the corner of his eye, Finn can see Alyssa look back at Pastor Sawyer for a second, wave her hand in apology, and rush out the office to make the call. Tension quickly floods the room, threatening to drown all inside. Daniel, barely able to keep afloat, instinctively starts to swim to safety at the water's edge, turning his body away from the desk.

"Daniel, why don't you go with her." The pastor suggests, seeming to note Daniel's anxiety. "I'd like to speak with your brother alone, and Alyssa may need the support. Just in case." *Talk to me alone? We've already gotten the alibi we needed, just let us go.* Finn thinks. "What could we possibly have to talk about?" Finn finally spits out, ire chained to every word. "Like you said, there are more important things to worry about than our pasts."

The pastor lets out a quick laugh to himself as he places his elbows on the table and clasps his hands. "As far as I'm concerned, that's not true anymore. God put you in front of me for a reason Finn, and it's time for us to figure out why."

Finn balls his fists and starts to grind his teeth. He can feel the skin of his face flush with blood, and heat spring from his ears. *I'll kill you old man.* He thinks, just before a sharp nudge at his thigh calls his attention.

"Calm down, Finn. I'd hate for her to receive any bad news on her own, so I'll go. We'll come grab you once we hear something back from Aunt Holly." Daniel promises, as he slides out of his chair. Then, after flashing an apologetic smile to the pastor, he gives into his instincts and bolts out the door with the subtlety of a charging hippo.

"Daniel," The pastor shouts at the fleeing cabbie, "please shut the door behind you."

The room remains silent until Daniel closes the door behind him. "You think God put me here today?" Finn questions. "The only reason I'm here is because Alyssa tried to bring us to your little basketball game."

"And now you are here, stuck and alone with yours truly." The pastor muses. "Whether *you* think it was God or not, we are here. All of human history led to you standing in front of me today, fixated on your anger like I once was. I refuse to let you leave this room without doing all I can. I know firsthand how that bitterness can eat away at you and burrow itself into your very soul, corrupting it and turning you into someone you don't recognize." The pastor stands from his chair and walks around the desk. He moves the middle chair at the front of the desk and sits in the one Alyssa had been using just moments earlier. With a calm and inviting gaze, he gestures for Finn to sit.

There Finn is. Standing before the man whose legacy and goodwill he was trying to ruin. He, the snake in the garden, tempting the good people of Chula Vista with the fruit man was never meant to have. He, Jonathan Finn Sawyer, the "Jonny Appleseed", is being offered a seat before a man of God. A reformed demon, brought back to the light through the voice of an angel. For a moment, Finn sees his chance to snuff out the life he blamed for all his misfortune. The only thing that kept him from going through with it, at first, was the mission at hand: stay out of jail and keep Daniel safe. But with that instinctive urge came an epiphany. His need for revenge not only nearly killed himself, but put the person he cared about most in harm's way.

If I just chose to set aside my feelings, Daniel would never have suffered like that tonight. This entire situation is all my fault. And while he struggles to concede, he considers that maybe the pastor is right. Finn sits down, his eyes glued to his own feet. "Well, let's hear it. What do you want to say?" Finn asks, giving his best attempt at an even-tempered tone.

"Considering your situation, I'll get straight to the point." The pastor states, his body leaning toward Finn. "It's okay to feel angry, but make sure you aren't driven by that feeling. Your brother seems to think you are all he needs in this world to conquer it. Or at least live a happy life. You should focus on the love and trust that keeps you two together and that has allowed you to thrive in this world enough to climb out of the trenches and put you in a position to help others, like how you are willing and able to provide a roof for your aunt and her family."

"Really? Thanks for the advice. I feel all better now. Can I go?" Finn sarcastically replies.

The pastor sighs deeply and puts his hand on Finn's shoulder. "The first step to getting over your hate, is to let it out. Go ahead. Tell me everything that comes to mind. Every little thing that has hurt you."

The touch disgusts Finn, but he allows it to stay as he thinks of the pastor turning his own life for the better. He thinks of doing the same for himself and Daniel. But he also feels a vindictive joy of confessing every way he had been hurt to Pastor Sawyer, knowing that it would cause the holy man's insides to squirm. Two birds, one stone.

"You want to know, huh?" Finn sickly laughs, raising his head to the ceiling. "Fine. I hope you've got a strong stomach." Finn relays a tale of abandonment, poverty, and abuse. A song of death and misfortune created from lyrics of desperation and carried on a melody of greed. The words spew from Finn like a broken faucet; he doesn't think about what words flow out, merely picturing the sickening highlight reel. He can't tell how much time is passing, but he also doesn't care. Oddly enough, he enjoys the release more than anything else he has felt in years. Finn only tells two lies over the course of his story - lies of omission. First: Finn never once claims to have had siblings other than Daniel. Second: he never reveals their true reason for moving to Chula Vista.

"After everything, we went to visit my mom in prison and she told us we had family here in Chula Vista. That's why we decided to move here, but it seems like we brought our misfortune with us." Finn concludes at the end of the macabre tale.

The pastor sits shocked, clearly taken aback by the extent Finn had suffered. To the extent Daniel had suffered, and yet still chose to smile. "After all that, you two still move forward. You're strong. Stronger than most." The pastor finally admits, shocking Finn who looks away from the ceiling and back at the pastor. "God has a plan for you two, of that I'm certain."

Feeling oddly relieved, Finn laughs. "You really think so? That's what you got from the story?" He questions. *Too bad you weren't around when I was growing up. I sure could have used that positivity of yours.* Finn thinks.

"Of course. You're here. I believe this church is a special place, and special people are called to it. Then, there is what you've been through. Suffering in this life is meant to make people stronger and put them on the correct path, and as I said, here you are." The pastor points up toward the roof of the church, not a shred of doubt tainting his words. "Everyone who enters these walls must make a choice. To climb and reach the greatness planned for them or sink deeper into despair."

Climb or sink? Finn considers. "As much as I dislike this unsolicited counseling, I like the sound of being bound for greatness." Finn finally responds.

Then the knock of two quick strikes to the wooden door clamors into the room, interrupting his next thought.

"Pastor Sawyer, it's getting late and the parking lot is clear. Alyssa has already spoken with her mother and explained they won't be staying here, so it's time for them to leave so we can close up." An icy voice rings with an otherworldly authority.

"Is that the famous harpy?" Finn asks, unbothered by the demand, and refusing to follow the orders of someone he's never met.

"Making jokes now, I see. Glad you are in a better mood." Pastor Sawyer laughs. "That is our famously stern Ms. Lucero, yes." The pastor stands and rubs the back of his head. "I apologize for cutting our conversation short, Finn, but Ms. Lucero is right. It's about time for her to lock up the church and address our new guests to explain the rules for staying here."

"No worries, spilling my guts made me a bit sick of the place anyway." Finn admits as he stands to his feet, lowering his sunglasses to finally look the pastor in the eyes for the first time. "But I have to say, it's like throwing up after a night of drinking; I feel a bit better. For Daniel's sake, I'll keep your advice in mind, Father."

PASTOR NICHOLAS SAWYER

"As I explained earlier, I'm not a priest." Nicholas laughs. *His eyes look awfully familiar. Not like Alyssa's or her brother's though. Holly, maybe?* Nicholas wonders with an entertained grin.

Finn slides his shades back over his sharp, olive eyes. "I know, I just like the sound." Finn chuckles as he turns toward the door, raising his hand to stop Nicholas from following. "You mind just hanging back? Your face kind of makes me sick right now since I opened up to you and all. I'm sure Alyssa or Ms. Lucero can show us out."

Ouch. Well, at least the young man is honest. May as well reply in turn. "Don't worry, I'm tired of staring into those shades anyway. Good night, my child." Nicholas jokingly replies, imitating a priest, before switching to a more serious tone. "Please have Alyssa and her mom update us on the situation. I'm praying for you all."

Finn leaves the room without saying a word, but waves a hand back at the pastor in acknowledgement as he leaves through the doors and saunters off with his family, trailed by Silvia who follows to lock the doors behind them.

Nicholas falls back into his chair and lets out a breath he didn't realize he was holding. *Please Lord, keep that family under your loving protection and allow them to receive all of the blessings that are meant to be theirs if they follow the correct path.* Pastor Sawyer stands to his feet and cracks his neck. *I've done all I can today, may as well head to bed now that I have the chance.*

Nicholas enters his room through the door at the back of the office, and places a "Do Not Disturb" sign on the door. As Silvia occasionally enters his office to grab documents or other resources while he sleeps, the sign is present to prevent her from knocking on his bedroom unless there is an emergency.

Nicholas prepares himself for bed, laying down in less than five minutes; falling asleep even quicker than it took to get ready. The sleep should be a peaceful, mute darkness that allows his brain to recharge. Free of stimulants to analyze and interpret.

Yet, unable to take his mind off Finn's story and the tragedies of Alyssa's family, the thought to open his eyes comes to the pastor. But, when he does, gone is his small, messy room. In its stead is a woman he hadn't seen in twenty or so years.

A one-week fling who let him use her bed and eat her food while he was drifting through town. Of course, on the day he finally grew bored of her, it was time to leave. On his way out, despite claiming to have fallen for the girl just that same morning, he stole her cash and jewelry, leaving without a word.

Nicholas is used to dreaming about the people he hurt. They normally look down on him and condemn him for all that he has done. For the audacity to help others, after spreading so much pain. But those were friends and old colleagues.

This woman was just a nameless few nights of passion, coming back to haunt him. She stands with her arms crossed, watching him in awe and gratefulness. The freckles on her cheeks sink into the pits of her dimples as her thin red lips curl into a smile. Voluminous, dirty-blonde hair drapes over her shoulders, guiding Nicholas's eyes to her body. And, just like he remembers, her figure is to die for, a necessity in her line of work.

"Hurry up and get ready, you'll be late for school." The woman notes sweetly at the pastor. Confused, Nicholas looks down and around him, noting that he is shorter than usual and that his hands and feet are tiny.

What is going on? Nicholas thinks before a voice cries out in reply.

"I'm going, Mom. I'm going!" States an unphased voice that seems to emanate from Nicholas' very lips.

The pastor attempts to cover his mouth out of shock, but his hands won't move. He is a passenger, not the pilot. His body zips past the mother and out a door that constructs itself out of nothingness. On the other side, he finds himself inside of a hospital, rushing down a hall.

"Which room?" A familiar, young girl's voice screams through his lips as Nicholas' vision passes room after room, dodging hospital staff that are reaching out to stop the mad dash. Then Nicholas feels his body jerk to a halt, submitting to a bear hug from behind.

"Calm down, Alyssa! You can't go in there." The officer chastises.

"Which room is he in? Tell me where my dad is!" The young Alyssa screams, her voice accompanied by tears the pastor can feel rolling down his face.

The officer tosses his captee into a chair and stands in front of them to keep them from getting up. "Stay put. The doctors are doing all they can. You have to keep calm and wait."

Nicholas looks up at the officer, tears still flowing; Alyssa's anguish and ire fill his mind. Then, as their right arm reaches up and wipes the salty rivers, the scene changes before Pastor Sawyer once again.

The heat that made the previous anger known was replaced by the sting of fresh wounds. He could feel blood trickling from his bottom lip, and his left eye was swollen shut. A breath-stealing kick to his gut strikes him without warning, leaving him nauseous and fetal on the floor, kissing the cold cement ground.

"You really thought I'd let you get away with talking back? I guess you got a little cocky since I pretended not to notice your disrespectful looks." A coarse, uncaring voice mocks. "You better learn to fall in line like the other kids and be grateful I let you all live here. All of you are just repurposed byproducts. You're trash that no one else wants, especially now that your mom went and got herself arrested. Now fix your damn face and get to work." The voice above him yells, its disembodied footsteps fading into the distance.

In covert defiance, his right arm is slammed against the ground, but instead of hard cement, his fist is met with prickly, itchy grass. Again and again, the fist pulverizes the green blades, as a young Alyssa's agonizing cry blasts with each blow. For what feels like hours, the earth is beaten, until a hand gripping at their shoulder brings the tirade to an end.

"Alyssa, stop! You're scaring your brother!" A broken Holly's voice informs. "I know it's hard, but you have to be strong right now. Your brother needs you. I need you."

The pastor's view turns. For a moment he sees the funeral grounds that belong to Armonia, littered with men and women dressed in either all black or police uniforms, as his vision travels and focuses on Holly, Alyssa's mother. No words leave their lips, but a single thought in Alyssa's own voice blares through Nicholas's head as his sights remain unblinking at the mother, struggling to hold back tears.

I'll be strong, Dad. I'll keep them safe. Just you watch.

Nicholas feels his body stand as it glances back in front of them. There it was. The gravestone for Alyssa's father.

I'll be strong, Dad. I'll keep them safe.

Then the pastor's vision turns toward Holly once more, but his vision darkens, and the mother he had expected to see has disappeared. In fact, everyone is gone. Except for three men. One, is a well-dressed, Caucasian man who is built like a strongman. He is adorned with gold chains and a shiny watch. The other two are much less audacious, wearing matching black suits and sunglasses. The only thing that stands out about them are their matching x-shaped scars; one wears the three-inch wide, skin-deep badge on his cheek, while the other bears his mark on the front of his throat.

The younger looking of the two hands the muscular figure a bag, before they both leave, sliding into an unassuming vehicle and taking off into the distance. At that point the pastor's body starts approaching the man, and he realizes he has been transported to a park he does not recognize.

"I feel so left out. I'm the only one not wearing sunglasses, huh, Finn?" The man states.

That's the voice from earlier! Pastor Sawyer thinks. *And Finn? Alyssa's cousin?*

"Not that'd I'd want to fit in with a bunch of scrubs like you. This right here, is my new meal ticket. You and the other children will be distributing these, along with the usual stuff, from now on."

"What are they exactly?" The voice of a teenage Finn questions.

The pastor watches as the man's face twists in response. "If you needed to know, I'd have told you. Just make sure each of our customers receives one free. Tell them it's like opiates and LSD had a baby." The man states while opening the sack and peering inside. "It may not look like much, but apparently this is some strong stuff, and it only takes one to get hooked. After a round of free samples, we should be able to charge what we want." He concludes with an evil smile.

This bastard just doesn't know. Finn's thoughts announce, reverberating through the pastor's mind. "I understand. I'll take care of it."

"Good." The man states as he tosses the bag to Finn. "Now, get out my face. I've got other business to attend to. I'll tell your mom you said hello."

"Thank you, Dad." Finn chimes as Nicholas feels his mouth curve into a forced smile. *What could he want with mom? He hasn't visited her in years.* Finn opens the sack and finds what looks to be hundreds of seeds. *What the hell is all this?* He thinks as he takes one out and admires it.

At that moment, Finn's scrawny hand morphs into the strong, calloused palm of Alyssa, the seed remaining pinched between her fingers.

"I knew it!" The girl declares aloud, hastily covering her mouth and looking over her shoulder after the outburst. *This looks just like the seed I found in mom's pocket the other month. The same seed Jacob has been bragging about selling at school. I can't believe mom is taking this stuff.* The girl thinks, tucking the seed into her pocket, and throwing her mom's coat back into the closet.

"What are you doing in mom's closet?" A young boy's voice asks.

Alyssa jumps but keeps her cool. "Girls just borrow each other's clothes sometimes. Was hoping to find a nice coat, but no luck." She lies.

"Okay, well what is that?" The boy questions, pointing to Alyssa's pocket that held the seed.

Alyssa looks down at her pocket and reaches in, showing its contents to her brother and prepared to lie about the "simple" seed.

"This, is your next big project." The coarse voice of Finn's *dad* responds. Nicholas' vision darkens once more, and he recognizes the frames of Finn's shades dampening his vision.

"I need you to reverse engineer whatever this stuff is made of. And since I need a chemist to do that, and your nephew here already works for me, I thought it was time to pull you into the family business. As this kid's uncle, you should be ecstatic to help his stepfather. And, if we can come to an arrangement, I could make you a very rich man." Finn's stepfather offers.

Nicholas' eyes dart between the drug peddler and Finn's apparent uncle; a man with a short, scraggly beard and a neatly-pressed, orange polo. His once-white coat is covered in small stains.

"Like I care about your money. I asked you what it is. Where did you get your hands on it? What does it do?"

"You sure ask a lot of questions for a scrawny guy in a lab coat." Finn's stepfather responds, cutting off the chemist, Finn's uncle.

"And you don't respond to enough of them, especially for someone that needs *me* to figure out what it is." Finn's uncle responds, causing Finn to shrink at the non-compliant response.

"You dragged me out of the lab, without letting me so much as remove my coat, so don't waste my time."

"Come again?" The baffled gorilla asks. "You think *you* can talk to *me* that way?"

"Of course. I'm not the same powerless kid who watched his sister marry some two-bit drug dealer that was sure to abuse her and her two-year-old child. You can't hurt me; you need me now. And if you were to hurt Finn, I'd never help scum like you." The chemist pauses for a moment, raising his hand to his chin and stroking his mustache. "Then again, Finn is about to graduate high school soon, isn't he? If I don't give you what you want, I'm assuming the boy loses his usefulness for you."

What is he thinking? He's going to get me killed with this nonsense. Finn thinks as he grits his teeth. He stares at his uncle with contempt, wishing he would just bend to his stepfather's will.

"Here is *my* proposal. I'll do what you ask, but Finn will be my assistant. I have other research projects that need to be completed, and the extra hands will get what you need done faster. Plus, that'll get him off the streets like I want, and he'll be able to keep an eye on me for you. I'll just tell the other department heads it's a shadowing program." Finn's uncle states, finally finishing his thought.

"Fine by me. Like you said, the boy is well past his useful years anyway. I just use him to care for the other kids now so their mothers can work more. Daniel can take over that job."

The uncle clicks his teeth. "Don't talk about your illicit business practices in my office. Now, get out, and leave Finn. After my class tonight, I'll have him explain everything I need to know, and we'll create a research plan together. He'll let you know if and when any other samples are needed."

Finn's stepfather laughs and stands to his feet. "It must be awfully hard to stand with those huevos you've grown." He steps away from the wooden desk and Finn watches as he heads to the door of the tiny office. As he reaches for the door, he turns around. "I'm glad we were able to strike a deal. Make daddy proud, Finn." He opens the door and exits with a slam, causing a framed diploma to fall and shatter against the floor. Glass litters the ground; tiny cubes that were sharp as daggers.

Why is this my life? Finn wonders.

"Damned brute." Finn's uncle complains as he gets up and grabs a small broom and dustpan from under his desk. He walks around the table and begins to sweep up the glass. "You're eighteen, right? Shouldn't you be close to finishing high school?"

Finn silently nods, rigid as a board. Nicholas can feel his tension. His fear of not only saying too much and ruining his stepfather's plan, but the safety his uncle had given him.

"Nice. If your grades are any good, why don't you apply here? I'll take care of your tuition and everything if you get in. How's that sound?" Finn's uncle proposes as he bends down to clean up the hazard.

"I can't attend school. What about Daniel and the rest of the kids? What would they do without me?" Finn questions, weary of the kind offer from his distant uncle.

"Well, you'll need a good reason to keep shadowing me, right? Becoming a student here is exactly how you can stick with that gorilla's plans and continue with our research past the end of high school. It will probably take a year or so." Finn's uncle turns and smiles at his nephew. "I finally have a way to get you out of his grasp. I promise to give you all the tools you'll need to finally be free, to free all of you, if you're willing to follow my lead."

Finn looks down and into the dustpan filled with shards, mesmerized by the proposal. He gets up from his chair and bends down to help pick up the larger pieces of glass. "Tell me." He finally says. "Tell me what you need me to do." Finn finishes, his voice resonating with Alyssa's as the scene shifts once more, and the pastor once again finds himself playing the role of the troubled teen.

"What do you need me to do? I'll do anything if you just stop selling to my mother!" Alyssa screams, blood gushing from her palm as she stands. Shards of broken glass from a carelessly discarded bottle, that broke upon impact when she was pushed onto her back and tried to catch herself, chew and sting her flesh with every movement. "She's not the same anymore. She hit and threatened my brother just because she thought he stole the seed you sold her. Every month it's the same. The first two weeks are bliss, and the next two are hell. She's all me and my brother have, and we just want to get her some help, and that starts with her getting off your drugs.

"It's too late for that. These seeds are the real deal. One is enough to make you addicted for life." Jacob states, towering over Alyssa. "Your mom made her choice. She prefers the false happiness seeds can offer, over you and your little family."

Alyssa's eyes shoot open at the revelation, disgusted by the lack of humanity. "And you just continue to sell those drugs, knowing what it can do to people?"

"Listen here, Alyssa. I give explicit instructions on what my product can do to each person, and how often you can take it in order to avoid overdose. That includes your mom. You can't stop me, or her." Jacob proclaims.

For a moment, Alyssa just stands, silent ; a chilling peace before the storm. "People like you just keep taking from my family. First, my dad. Now my mom. No amount of begging in the world will convince you if the law can't. I should have realized that sooner." Alyssa muses as she plants her feet, clenching her wounded fist while reaching into her jacket pocket with her left hand. She can feel the unforgiving shards digging into her palm and fingers as she takes a deep, life affirming breath.

"What? Finally given up?" Jacob mocks. "Good, I've gotta go. I have to warm up with the guys before Midnight starts."

Then, Alyssa whips out her father's old revolver from the inner pocket of her varsity jacket. "No. You're not leaving. I'll do whatever it takes to protect my family. I promised dad." She states, plain as day and without a hint of remorse. Alyssa's spirit burns with purpose, and a sick demon of joy creeps into the hearth of her soul as Jacob's face twists into terror. "How did you put it? You made your choice?" Alyssa mocks before shooting Jacob in the shoulder.

Jacob begs for her to stop. He begs her to let him live, revealing that he is only a proxy. The real kingpin is a man who goes by Jonny Appleseed. Yet, he refuses to give up his boss's location, even as he is shot in one of his legs, each time Alyssa's demands are ignored. Repeatedly, he screams that he, too, is on the seeds and needs them to live; but to Alyssa, these are just the cries of a desperate addict. The pleas fall on deaf ears, as Jacob bleeds to death, on the ground.

Alyssa picks up Jacob's phone and uses his, still warm, finger to unlock it. "You should have just told me, Jacob. Why didn't you just tell me?" She whispers, holding back tears.

The dark alleyway transforms into a chemistry lab filled with tubes and beakers that are neatly placed along the benches. As if an experiment was about to take place. Jacob's fresh body on the floor, became another's dressed in a stained, white lab coat. A man dressed in a simple, all black suit can be seen kneeling over the corpse. The man stands, revealing his distinctive, x-shaped scar across the bridge of his nose as he walks toward the pastor's vision.

"Please tell me you won't be as difficult. My orders were to kill all those involved in the attempted infringement on my boss's intellectual property. That would be your uncle, the chemistry professor, and your stepfather who made the deal to sell the seeds for us under our guidelines. While your uncle here may not have been privy to them, they both broke the guidelines when your stepfather tried to have your uncle reverse engineer the seeds. But you're just a kid and I have no intention of ending your life if you can tell us what we need. If not though, I will assume you are lying and complicit. You will be killed like your uncle here. Just my boss's policy. I'm sure you understand."

Finn remains silent, unsure of what to say next. His hands tremble and his stomach twists into a knot. *I am a curse.* He thinks as he stares at his uncle's drained body.

"For the sake of your siblings, you may want to answer my question now. I have a colleague who should have infiltrated your home by now and he's been instructed to question the children and kill your stepfather, but unlike me he won't ask twice. He's young and impatient. That doesn't bode well for your brothers and sisters."

Without hesitation, Finn reveals to the killer where his stepfather's stash of seeds are. The man, referring to himself as Ar, relays the location to his junior. The colleague, who he refers to as Zeta, confirms once he finds the hidden storage.

"Now what about Daniel and the others? Are they okay?" Finn rushes to question as soon as he sees the positive nod from Ar. *Please, they have to be okay.*

Ar simply hangs up the phone and places it in his pocket. "My colleague was able to make it into your home much quicker than I anticipated, so his questioning also began sooner. Only one is left. Daniel. The others are dead. My apologies." He states as he turns to leave the lab, slicking back any potential stray, nut-brown hairs.

"You should leave and pick up your brother before our cleanup crews arrive. I have the freedom of discretion, they do not. Per instructions they'll treat you and your brother as witnesses and kill you both if they find you on the scene."

Finn, quick to react, barrels out the lab and pushes past Ar, heading straight down the hall and toward his car so he can get to Daniel. *There's no way everyone is dead. There's no way."*

As soon as Finn slides into his seat, once again, the pastor finds himself in the body of Alyssa as she pulls up to a large home in West Lake. *I think this is the place. I'll just park in front and dump the car here.*

Time to make this bastard pay.

Finn's and Alyssa's voices harmonize. The home shifts into the shape of Armonia Church, and the neighborhood collapses away. The pastor is in the body of Finn as he stares daggers at the holy sanctuary.

"What do you mean?" Daniel questions. "I thought we were going to come down here for his help. Mom said she was sure he was a changed man now and that he'd be happy to help."

"Such a good man that he could fix up this town. Bringing peace between gangs, creating youth programs. Even starting a damned school." Finn clenches his fist. "But, not once did he come and help out his son. Not once did he come up and help our mom! He let us rot up there like forgotten plants in the corner. Screw his help. He could have changed our lives for the better a long time ago and he chose not to, so I'm going to use all the grime he allowed us to wallow in to bring this town back to its knees."

"Finn, let's just think about this for a moment. We didn't move all the way down here for revenge. We moved to start a new life." Daniel says.

"I've been thinking for a long time, Daniel. Two whole months. I'll do whatever it takes to cripple this man's legacy. With that said, now that we've got you settled, here's my new address." Finn states as he turns and hands Daniel a piece of paper.

"You got an entire new house without telling me first? How did you afford it? What is it for? What are you planning?"

Finn smiles and removes his shades as he looks Daniel in the eyes. "If you're in danger, come see me. But anything short of that, just call me. I don't know what I'd do If I lost you too. Probably just curse the world and end it all. It's better for everyone if you stay away and live the normal life you always wanted." Finn advises with a loving firmness as a beat-up, gold sedan pulls up to them in the parking lot and Finn jumps in.

At that moment, the pastor connects the dots. Finn's familiar eyes, the nameless fling, Finn's story, and the visions he had witnessed. *What have I done?* Nicholas cries, shattering the dream and leaving the pastor back in his own body.

Prisms of light swirl before his eyes as they pull away and fly to the center of the dark cavern he finds himself in. He can feel the moist, warm ground beneath him squish with every movement as he gets up to his feet. The prisms collect into a twisting colony of rotating light, forcing itself into the shape of a man with the head of a giant, elongated prism. The creature kneels and sticks its outstretched finger into the moist, bloody floor.

The pastor instantly recognizes the creature, and screams "Silvia, Silvia!" at the top of his lungs. *It can't be. This isn't possible.*

The pastor screams. "Silvia! Silvia! Silvia!" He screams until the heavens themselves open up, revealing a golden cross dangling in the sky, from a slender golden chain. The ground beneath him quakes, causing the gelatinous surface to gyrate and slosh. And then, he's awake, staring at the very cross that was just descending from the sky. The cross Silvia wears on her necklace. He looks further up and grabs Silvia by the shoulder, peering into her penetrating, raven eyes.

"I've seen it, Silvia. I've seen it." He states, pausing only because of the pain in his chest. His panicked screams had left him breathless.

SILVIA LUCERO

"Breathe. Settle down Nicholas, you'll worry our guests. Now, what did you see?" Silvia calmly inquires.

"The prisms of light your mother wanted you to inherit. The visions they bring." Nicholas reveals, never breaking eye contact. "I saw, El Brillo."

PRISM 3: PART 1

FRIGID LIGHT

SILVIA LUCERO

Instantly, Silvia delivers a reprimanding chop to Nicholas's forehead, causing his olive eyes to squint. As he falls back on his pillow, wincing from the quick blow, she stands and turns to face the door. "You called me over because you had a nightmare? Nicholas, you're over forty years old." She chastises.

"But, it was so real." Nicholas asserts, while rubbing his head. "I could see everything that young man, Finn, told me about and more; just as if I had possessed his body and witnessed it myself. Through those olive eyes." Nicholas's voice rings like a faint memory Silvia had tucked away long ago, but never forgotten. "I could see everything Alyssa went through after her father died too." Nicholas swallows out of hesitation. "I even witnessed Alyssa, murdering Jacob Yoon." Nicholas summarizes with a shaky, anxious breath.

Silvia stands quietly, her back still turned away from Nicholas. She searches for the best way to calm her old friend's spirits. "You had just listened to Finn's unfortunate tale, and Alyssa was the one who brought him to you. I'm sure that family's constant misfortune was on your mind as you fell asleep; you dreamed about things you already knew about, simple as that." Silvia states, making her leave. "In regard to murder, I'm certain you are just worried about Jacob Yoon since he's never missed the games before. As intense as she is on the field, I can't picture Alyssa killing anyone, let alone the captain of her Judo Club."

"But Silvia, hear me out. Just think about this for a second." Nicholas begs. "After all of that, I saw the creature from your mother's stories: a hive of floating prisms. They gave off a blinding, frigid light. It numbed my skin in an instant. How can you explain that away?"

Silvia stops halfway through the threshold of the door. "If you truly saw El Brillo, it means my mother is dead. Do you think El Brillo would reach you, by chance, before news of my mother's passing reached me?" She questions, a tinge of annoyance in her cold voice. "Of course not."

Then, fighting the urge to look back, concerned about what effects such visions could leave on her old friend, she adds in a still-stern, but marginally softer tone "Nicholas, I'm very busy right now, so unless you have anything more to add, I'm

going to continue getting everyone settled. Pray on it, Pastor
Nicholas, and go to sleep.

She closes Nicholas's door without allowing him to reply,
and quickly hustles over to the room of her newest
admission. Just after shutting the large office doors, Silvia stops
and closes her eyes. *A frigid light? There's just no way. First
Aurelio and now her? It's impossible.* She refutes, biting her
thumbnail as the possibility of the pastor's dream being
something more bores deeper into her psyche. She looks over to
the door closest to her left, and for a moment reconsiders. *But if
what she's told me is true, I can't ignore Nicholas's dream.*

Silvia calms her breath, turning her mind to the tragic
story that the church's newest guest had divulged to Silvia,
seeking to explain her sudden appearance and secure Silvia's aid.
Silvia breathes in and out rhythmically, focusing on every detail
of the story, as her mother's old tales suggested. Then the images
come.

Silvia finds herself staring at the familiar sight of the sun, tucking itself behind desert hills and olive trees from a window, as night falls.

The noise of a loud engine and tires bumping on uneven terrain distract her, and she notices as two men in a dark gray jeep speed through the single lane, dirt road to enter the village Silvia once called home, Dos Ojos. A collection of twenty or so homes that sat just miles away from city. The archway marking the entrance shakes as the jeep thunders by with bass laden hip-hop.

Two men stroll out of the SUV, rolling up their sleeves to reveal their tattoos of the macabre. They demand to see the curandera in the black bandages.

Dara Lucero strolls confidently toward the obtrusive visitors as the jet-black skirt of her traje de tehuana, adorned with bright yellow and red flowers, flows with the gentle breeze of the wind. "Why would Aurelio bring her out? What is he thinking?" A confused, female voice, not her own, mumbles from Silvia's lips.

Without hesitation, a woman whose face is enveloped in onyx cloth exits the home in the center of the village, guided by a short-bearded man in his forties, wearing a dusty, red plaid shirt and a cowboy hat. It's Silvia's mother, Dara Lucero, walking arm in arm with Aurelio, Silvia's elder brother.

Just as the stolen words fly out, the memory warps. Silvia now finds herself on the ground and straddled by one of the men, struggling against his grip. Immediately, the other starts to pull out his gun. Silvia feels defiant anger build up in her core as she stares down her shooter-to-be, but the gunshot never comes. Only a fatal, muted gasp as the man is stabbed from behind by a hero in a brown sweater.

Hearing his partner's cry and noticing a blood covered knife in the hand of his assailant, the man leaps off, and runs back to the jeep, swearing he will return with the monstrous, scarred men that hired them to track down the bandaged curandera. As he shakes his fist in disdain, Dara Lucero merely states, ["Bring them if you must, but you will not get what you seek when you do."]

Suddenly, Silvia is blinded by an abrasive black whirl that itches at her skin. Though without sight, she can feel a stinging pain in her soles. Hours of wear birthing blistering sores. But more than that, she feels the loving guidance of a firm palm, that helps her body to push forward. Then, Silvia hears Aurelio call back, demanding they halt. "Do you see those eyes, Emmanuel? In the brush?"

Once the man has sped off, the woman known as La de Las Vendajes tells the entirety of the town that no matter what they do, La Banda will return to kill them all. ["Those that can, move in with a relative as far away as possible. Those that work in the city, find a new home and pretend you have never heard of Dos Ojos. Those that have nowhere else to go? Run. Follow Aurelio, find Silvia."]

His observation is met with a disorienting, screeching warble from above mixing with the murderous melody of bullets sowing into the flesh of the poor souls of their group. Silvia can hear every scream of terror. Every plea for salvation; prayers to save them from the Devil's Hound. She feels' her guide's hand grip hard and then loosen before falling from her own as he screams for her to hide. "Querida, Escondete!"

Silvia hears the soft thud his body makes as he lands on the desert brush. Then the veil before her is torn away by her own hands, and Silvia can now see a man in a brown sweater, gripping his right side as blood slips through the spaces between his fingers. And while Silvia does not recognize the man, her heart aches, pining for his salvation. "Emmanuel! No!" Her lips scream.

An automated cap lowers into place, sealing the truck bed and plunging the world into darkness.

As the sound of bullets and the warbles come to an end, Silvia can feel the sleeve of her dress gripped from behind as she is yanked by a scarred hand and thrown into the back of a midnight blue pickup truck.

Silvia opens her eyes, finding herself in the hall of the Armonia church, just outside the pastor's office doors. For a moment, Silvia dismisses the scene as her own imagination going wild, but the visceral nature of the scenes, the feel of the grass and blood between her fingers, as she held the familiar yet unknown lover, led her to the only conclusion.

Memories that aren't my own. Not only are Nicholas's fears warranted, but it looks like our new guest isn't telling me the whole story. Silvia thinks, grinding her teeth as her body grows hot with anger. She approaches the door leading to the author of the truncated tale, but pauses to calm her soul. *Don't blame her Silvia. There must be a reason.*

After stifling the storm inside, Silvia knocks on the thick wood leaf of the door leading to her guest and pushes it open as she twists the knob at the same time. As soon as there is enough space for her to squeeze through, Silvia swings to the other side, shuts the door, and locks it in the same motion. "Sorry about the interruption. Now, where were we?"

"¿Todo va bien?" A worried voice questions from the bed on the opposite side of the room. A bed the voice's owner was more than happy to call hers, even if only for a night.

"Sí, Sí." Silvia pauses for a moment, searching for the right way to interrogate her guest further. "Mira, antes de ir al hospital, hay algo que no entiendo. ¿Para qué te dejó viva ese Padraig? ¿Te dijo, Malena?"

Malena, wearing a white, Armonia hoodie that belongs to Silvia, paired with borrowed navy-blue jeans and white sneakers that were a bit loose on her feet no matter how she tied them, looks up, but Silvia avoids her gaze, focusing instead on the triple knotted laces. "¿Por qué te importa ahora? Hace unos minutos estabas lista para lidiar con este Padraig y sus demonios. Para ayudarme con este dispositivo en el cuello y salvar a Emmanuel." Malena angrily replies while pointing at her neck.

Silvia shifts her eyes to the area she points to, remembering the tiny scab that was hidden by Malena's thick hair. "Sí, pero en el caos debía haber algo de ti que le llamó la atención. Ya que, en el principio, quería operarte el ojo y no a Emmanuel." Silvia questions, hoping that her prodding would give her the answers she needed to finish the edges of this puzzle. "Pero, Malena, como te dije, deberíamos hablar inglés. Most of our guests are immigrants as well. If you want to try and keep our conversation as secret as possible, English is the way to go, ironically."

Malena rolls her eyes and scoffs, but complies. "Where are you going with this? I don't see how this helps save Emmanuel."

"I need to make sure this doesn't extend beyond our village, La Banda, and your kidnapper. And I can't make a plan without knowing the scope of the situation and understanding this devil's mind." Silvia replies cooly.

"Still so pragmatic, even when it comes to your own family and village. You just found out your brother is dead, and that your childhood friend is in danger. Why can't you just help like a normal person would?" Malena questions sarcastically.

"Says the woman who doesn't seem scared one bit to fight back against someone she called a mad scientist." Silvia pointedly responds with a restrained chuckle.

Malena smiles slightly and leans back with both her arms pressed into the mattress behind her and looking toward the ceiling. "I guess we're both weird, but maybe that's what we'll need if we are going to save Emmanuel and kill that red-headed bastard."

She really is doing her best to incriminate me and the church. Silvia bemoans as her eye twitches at Malena. *But she's not wrong. Someone that dangerous can't be allowed to live and get his way. Though I'm not sure Emmanuel is still alive, poor thing.* "Please Malena, tell me. Why did he leave you alive?"

Malena glances away from the ceiling and toward Silvia, staring bronze daggers of displeasure into her soul. But the daggers were just a smokescreen covering the true emotion that swam in her gaze: guilt that Silvia notices clear as day. "I don't see why it matters, but he said it was because my eyes were covered with black bandages."

MALENA ZÁRATE IGNACIO

Malena leers at her childhood friend that should feel like a stranger to her, but is still the same old Silvia. The same girl that left home at twelve, determined to create a safer route for women, children, and families seeking to cross the border; a calculating, obsidian-eyed eagle with a terrifying sense of justice, guided by a passion for doing right in this world. Just like her mother. *That must be why she chose her.* Malena thinks.

"Black bandages? Like mother's? Why would you have those around your eyes?" Silvia interrogates as questions pop into her head.

Malena rolls her eyes and rubs her forehead out of frustration as Silvia walks up and sits to her right. "Remember when I told you that your mother ordered Aurelio to bring us to you, so we could escape the vengeance of La Banda?" She asks, turning her head to the left and toward the window that hangs above the bed.

"Of course, she even reminded you all of her favorite idiom. 'Good is innate. Bad acts can be corrected. But Evil must be slain or avoided.' Under the threat of La Banda, all you could do was run."

"You and her are of the same mind. Yes, that's exactly what she demanded of us. But not just Aurelio, Emmanuel, and myself were told to run; it was the entire village. Though only nine of us were leaving Mexico entirely, everyone was told to evacuate the village forever."

Malena strokes her left eye, where quick dashes by a surgical pen had once been hours earlier. *I guess it's time to come clean.* "Everyone quickly listened, and Aurelio began to gather supplies for the trip with the others who were planning to cross the border. Everyone except me and Emmanuel. Your mother told me and Emmanuel to come to her home. There was a gift she wanted to give you, that I needed to take for her. Your inheritance."

"My inheritance?" Silvia asks, a slight tremble in her normally serene and commanding voice betraying her fear.

"Yes. The only thing of value that Dara Lucero kept in Dos Ojos: El Brillo." Malena pauses for a moment, remembering the odd exchange. "When we reached her home, she ordered Emmanuel to stay outside as she brought me into her dark home. She lit two candles at the side of a large chair in the corner of the room and then sat down." Malena grips her chest as her breath grows labored at the memory. "Then she removed those bandages that had covered everything except her mouth and nostrils for as long as I could remember."

"And what did you see?" Silvia questions abruptly. Malena can feel the bed shift as Silvia's outburst reaches her ears. *I guess even her own children have never seen her face before.*

"Honestly, she's beautiful. At first, I saw you, but ten years younger and with pure, black hair, darker than yours. If I had seen her on the city street, I'd have assumed she was some twenty-two-year-old on her way home from work or university. But that didn't shock me; given her many nicknames. It was what happened when she opened her eyes that threw me off.

I could only describe it as true darkness. A room graced with only two candles felt lit by the sun in comparison to Dara Lucero's eyes. Her irises floated in the darkness, letting not a single beam of light escape. I was entranced." Malena gasps for air, the memory stealing her breath.

"Then your mother stood up, told me to sit in the chair, and tied the bandages around my eyes. When she was done, she told me not to remove the bandages until I was face to face, and alone with you. Of course, I promised her I never would."

Malena can feel her eyes well up with tears as she grips the covers tightly.

She turns to Silvia and finally reveals what she wanted to keep hidden until Emmanuel was safe and sound. "I'm sorry for hiding the whole truth earlier, Silvia. I'm so sorry. I was afraid you wouldn't help me if I told you that I messed up."

Silvia's face is blank, staring off to the door in disbelief. The tears clouding Malena's vision reach a tipping point, and begin their slow crawl down her cheeks. As she looks at Silvia's empty stare, she already knows. The look of shock had nothing to do with El Brillo potentially being lost. It was the fact that her mother had given it to Malena in the first place. It meant that her mother believed she would die soon, and La Joven Eterna, Dara Lucero, was never wrong.

Even if she fights to hide it, Malena is certain of the suffering and guilt Silvia feels for never having returned to the village in person after all these years. She knows Silvia wishes to mourn for her family and village. To cry and shut everything out. But knowing there is no time for such things, she presses on. "Then what happened? What happened when you left her home?

Silvia interrogates, lowering her head and looking toward the multi-colored carpet below.

"Nothing much happened after we left your mother's home. Emmanuel guided me to the edge of the village so we could meet up with Aurelio, my parents, and four others; newcomers to the village that decided to stay after receiving help from your mother a few years back. We..." Malena answers, dejectedly, pausing the moment Silvia gripped her the bottom trim of her blue, Armonia hoodie like a vice.

"My mother didn't go with you?" Silvia asks, filling in the silence, her grip tightening.

"Your mother y mis bisabuelos decided to stay. {'Despite my appearance, I'm old and tired. I'm sure Los Viejos feel the same. We ran from carnage once, a hundred years ago. Now I wish to die with the home I created with my friends all those years ago.'}" Malena states, giving her best impression of the matriarch of Dos Ojos.

Malena slides closer to Silvia, just inches away, and places feels her kind but pensive hand on her shoulders. "Your mother said it was a blessing to see her children leave the village and thrive in the world. Her greatest wish that her y mis bisabuelos begged the heavens for during the war had been granted, there was nothing more they needed to do here on this earth, except give you your inheritance." Malena divulges solemnly, as Silvia's misted, dark gaze meets her own.

SILVIA LUCERO

Silvia stares back at Malena, the now woman that her mother once claimed was the other side of her coin when they were children. Someone who she had never known to tell a lie, even to her detriment. Silvia understands the weight it must have put on Malena's soul, but she was willing to bear it for Emmanuel.

Silvia sits silently, and undoes her ponytail, allowing her raven hair to fall and cover her face. A poor attempt to cover the tears, soon to drop. Yet, the short curtain of black strands could never silence the accompanying sobs.

"We did our best to convince them to leave, but time was short and Aurelio had to lead not only a couple of elderly, but a woman blinded by bandages through the wilderness. We had to leave right away, so we obeyed our elders and left." Malena pauses for a moment, taking a deep breath. "Emmanuel said their faces were the saddest joy he'd ever seen. Like the prideful cry of a parent watching their child go off to university."

"Then what?" Silvia solemnly questions, not acknowledging the attempt at comfort.

"Then what? You basically already know the rest. Aurelio noticed the hawk in the sky, six hours into our trek. He said it had been following and circling us for well over an hour. 'Something is wrong, I don't care for that hawk circling over us.'

He said. But we kept on moving, not knowing what it meant. Then, about twenty minutes later, the demon dog came out of the brush and killed everyone." Malena grabs her chest, her arms shaking from the fresh wound of hearing everyone around her scream in terror, some choking and gurgling on their own blood as their cries went unanswered.

"In the chaos I failed your mother and looked Emmanuel in the eyes. I didn't want him to die; I wanted to try and save him. But the moment after I looked him in the eyes, the shots ended and the hawk went silent. Padraig approached us in his monstrous pickup and dragged me away before throwing me into the truck bed with the hound. Just after the cap shut, Emmanuel screamed for me. Padraig simply said, 'Come and get her if you want her, but I doubt you'd survive the hour-long walk in that shape. I live that way, so show me what you've got.' Then he left Emmanuel for dead."

"Did Emmanuel look Padraig in the eye, Malena?" Silvia asks.

Malena drops her arms, and holds the edge of the bed. "I don't know, I could only see that Devil mocking him. It is possible that he did, and Padraig passed El Brillo to another, but it's just as possible that Emmanuel died out there alone, and his sombra came to save me in his stead." Malena admits, her hand gripping the bed sheets tightly.

Silvia sits in silence for a moment before standing. "What did he look like when he came to rescue you?"

"He looked like he always had. Dark brown hair, and warm, chocolate eyes. He was pale, but I'm sure that's because he was still injured when he arrived."

Silvia turns and reaches down, wiping Malena's tears from her cheek as she contains her own. "El Brillo, as my mother told it, is an emotionless creature that hops from host to host on instinct. A mind and soul without a body to control or spirit to drive it, it goes collecting its hosts' knowledge and experience for the day it can finally walk the earth on its own; the day a host dies with it inside. Then, El Brillo heals the body and utilizes the spirit of its deceased host as their soul slumbers in wait for the end of days, becoming La Sombra. The process leaves the creature with the remaining desires and form of its host, while retaining its unfathomable knowledge. The only clues that a person has undergone this death and pseudo-revival are an inhuman timbre in their voice, obsidian hair, and sable eyes. The very eyes you saw when my mother removed her bandages."

"Where are you going with this?" Malena questions.

Silvia drags her hand down Malena's smooth cheek and positions it beneath her chin before gently raising Malena's tear-quenched bronze gaze to her own. "Emmanuel is alive. He is no shadow, but true living, breathing flesh and blood." Silvia pushes down the thought that her brother was dead, and her mother could be dead or dying as they speak. There were bigger issues that needed solving before she could mourn. "And we'll rescue him together and stop Padraig." She states with her smile she had been practicing for years; To most, an awkward, slightly off-putting smile, but one that she hopes her childhood friend will understand as a gesture of loving support.

MALENA ZÁRATE IGNACIO

"You'll still help? Even after I betrayed your mother's trust and lost El Brillo because of it? Even after I lied to you?" Malena asks in shock as she watches Silvia walk away after releasing her chin. "Why aren't you angry? I'd be yelling my head off in your position."

"Maybe, but you'd still understand that it was all to protect a loved one, and that you couldn't let your anger get in the way of helping someone. We're two sides of the same coin, after all." Silvia proclaims, her back still facing Malena. "Besides, in my position, you'd already know that El Brillo is here with us. And, if my count isn't off, I just returned it to you. We'll know for sure once we both sleep though."

"Wait, what? But what makes you think that?" Malena asks, touching her face in disbelief. *I could have sworn I...*

"Nicholas's nightmare." Silvia answers confidently. "It seems that sometime between you giving El Brillo to Emmanuel and tonight, El Brillo made its way to Nicholas. The memories he saw in his slumber, triggered by a visit he received just before heading to bed, caused a night terror..."

"And you think that's what caused the scream we heard earlier?" Malena finishes for Silvia, nearly screaming herself at the realization.

"That's right. He told me he had seen El Brillo, even though I had only mentioned it in passing over a decade ago. More importantly he described its light as 'frigid'. A detail I had never given him before, but matches mother's stories. With your arrival, I knew it couldn't have been a coincidence." Silvia thinks aloud, pausing only for Malena's response.

"But how did El Brillo get to your pastor?" Malena questions, doing her best to hide the glee in her voice at the revelation that El Brillo had returned home.

"Well, we know it didn't come from you. You avoided all contact with anyone except me ever since you left Padraig's home, correct?" Silvia seeks to confirm.

Malena nods her head, certain she hadn't interacted with anyone; not a word was shared, not a glance was flashed, another's way since she had left that devil's accursed den. "I kept my face hidden with the hood until the moment I found you."

"Well then, what happened between your departure and our esteemed pastor's nightmare is a mystery. I do have a theory." Silvia shares, caressing her own chin, before shrugging off the concern and raising her hands in nonchalant defeat. "But it doesn't truly matter. El Brillo has returned to us; we need to focus our efforts on thwarting Padraig's plans." Silvia declares as she unlocks the door and opens it. "The first step toward that is getting that tracker removed, so we should head out. My friend will be expecting us soon."

How could she not be concerned about El Brillo? What if there are sombra running around town with that devil's knowledge? Malena worries.

But her thoughts are interrupted as Silvia continues her speech. "But before we head to the van, let's head over to my room and find something to cover our eyes so we don't spread El Brillo carelessly. I should have some sunglasses…"

PRISM 3: PART 2

SUNGLASSES

MALENA ZÁRATE IGNACIO

"What good are sunglasses going to do?" Malena asks, incredulous of the eyewear's potential.

"We'll use them to cover our eyes, of course." Silvia responds matter-of-factly, checking the halls and then gesturing for Malena to follow. "Wearing bandages like my mother would be too conspicuous, and besides, neither of us can drive if we're blind."

"And what makes you think they'll work? If sunglasses could do the job, wouldn't your mother have worn them instead of the bandages for all these years?" Malena retorts, raising an eyebrow as she follows Silvia out the door and toward her room at the end of the hall near the entrance to the sanctuary.

"Well," Silvia whispers. "Our pastor, Nicholas, had three visitors this evening after the games were interrupted, just before going to bed; one of our students and two of her cousins. The student and one of the cousins left the room to allow the third to have a private conversation with Nicholas. This third individual was wearing sunglasses and..."

Malena squinches her eyes, and her thoughts fly through her teeth like a whip before the crack. "You want to wear sunglasses, because you saw some guy wearing them. That doesn't seem paper thin to you?" She shouts.

Silvia twists quickly, bringing her finger to her lips to quiet her friend. "Based on just that, it would be. But, you work with what you know, and I know two things for certain: That El Brillo transfers with eye contact, and that Nicholas is much too popular for him to have obtained El Brillo at Midnight Basketball. He would have spread it to any of the innumerable people that stopped him to chat." Silvia pauses for a moment, reaching her hand toward the doorknob as they reach her room. "No, it had to be one of the three, and my bet is that El Brillo was given to him by the last person to see him."

"Still feels flimsy to me. Like you said, why wouldn't the brillo have switched to another person at the basketball thing if they were also there." Malena spits out, tossing the logic back.

Silvia scratches her cheek playfully with the tip of her finger, responding with an annoying air of someone in the know. "They didn't get inside on time. They had just arrived in the parking lot when Nicholas called the tournament off and were

almost immediately whisked away to his office. No time to look
anyone in the eyes, except our pastor himself."

Malena looks at the side of Silvia's face in disbelief. "Let's
assume you're correct, and the glasses work. You're just going to
assume that he never took off his sunglasses while he was
outdoors? He could have received El Brillo from someone in the
parking lot."

"I'm not assuming, I know." Silvia asserts as she opens
her door. "Nesho, a boy Nicholas and I used to care for, told me
before he headed home with his mom. Apparently, Nicholas
briefly stopped to chat with them from across the lot while
leading the group to his office, so Nesho asked me if I knew
anything about the weird guy wearing sunglasses at night that
Pastor Nicholas was taking inside the church."

Silvia raises a finger to Malena, pausing her next thought.
"On that note, give me one second, the glasses should be in my
drawer. Everyone should be settled, but if you see anyone, just
avoid eye contact." She orders as she slips into her room like a
fox on the hunt.

Great to see she's as domineering as always. Malena
begrudges, wondering how she ever dealt with someone so high-
handed when they were children. But just as quickly as she left,
Silvia appears once more, rocking a pair of surprisingly chic,
butterfly sunglasses and shutting the door behind herself,
locking it with a key.

"Here you go!" She states with her icy, practiced smile,
offering Malena a pair with square lenses.

There's that smile again. When did she start doing that? Malena thinks as she reaches for the oversized, golden-squared frames. Los Luceros are known for their stern, nearly expressionless faces that belied their typically kind natures. "Thanks." She replies warmly, taking the glasses and throwing them over her face as she forewent the temptation to ask Silvia about this new, unheard of Lucero grin. "So again, why did you think they would work?

"Well, with Nesho's testimony, plus seeing him leave them on when I escorted all three out of the church, leads me to believe he couldn't have transferred it to anyone except Nicholas." Silvia answers as she gestures to Malena to follow her toward the sanctuary door.

Malena was slowly being brought over to Silvia's way of thinking, but still had one question remaining. "And you think this weird guy took off his sunglasses while he was speaking with the pastor. Why?"

"Why? That I'll probably never know. But Nicholas said his eyes were olive colored. The conversation was apparently very emotional, so I doubt the color of his eyes came up. That leads me to believe the last person he ever looked in the eyes before falling asleep, was our sunglass-wearing inspiration." Silvia announces as they pass through the sanctuary doors and venture toward the main entrance of the church.

"Okay…" Malena thinks aloud, finally conceding to Silvia's theory but unsure of how it would work long term. "So, we wear sunglasses for the rest of our lives?"

"Of course, not. Just whoever decides to keep El Brillo with them." Silvia whispers as they reach the front doors of the sanctuary that lead out into the parking lot.

Was that a joke? Malena thinks, certain the Silvia she knew would never seriously propose something so ridiculous.

"We'll talk more once we are in the van. We don't want your little friends listening in." She says, walking through the front doors.

Malena cuts her eyes and sighs, clicking her teeth with bitter submission. There is no telling what would happen if Padraig came to know of El Brillo, and Malena is well aware that the beasts constantly follow the chip embedded under the skin at the base of her skull. So, she silently treks behind Silvia, checking the parking lot for any signs of the mechanical hound.

There is no trace of its deathly, scarlet eyes, but the hawk still flies high above the church. Malena stops for a moment and points to the hawk, mouthing "I'll see you soon, bastard."

"Hurry, I've already texted my friend. He'll meet us in the parking garage in twenty minutes." Silvia orders, feigning impatience. Malena jogs over and hops into the Armonia branded, glossy blue van with Silvia, and they pull off, heading toward the hospital.

In the van, Silvia makes it clear that she has no intention of housing El Brillo, but that they should cross the bridge of what to do next with it when they get there. She reiterates that their only concerns are protecting Malena, saving Emmanuel, stopping

Padraig's schemes and returning to their village to save the remaining elders and Dara Lucero. And though Malena is uncomfortable with setting the topic aside completely, especially with potential sombras roaming around town, she too puts her husband and neighbors before El Brillo and agrees with the decision.

"So, what's the plan for after we get this tracker out of my neck, then?" Malena asks impatiently.

"There is no plan right now." Silvia states in a cool, teasing tone. "Let's start with what you know about Padraig's home."

Malena, eager to be more than a damsel in distress and play an active role in planning Padraig's downfall, springs up straight. "Well, after I was led out of the bastard's little shed, I scanned the back of Padraig's house and its surroundings to get a better understanding of where I was and where I should go. It was a pretty normal house from what I could tell, and only two things stuck out; The first was the young boy with red hair in a tiny window upstairs. He ducked down just as we nearly locked eyes, but he resembled Padraig for sure- had to be his son, the one he wanted me to kill as part of his sick deal. The second thing I noticed was the broken window at the front that Emmanuel must have used to break into the home when he arrived."

Malena pauses for a moment, recalling the split decision that may have extended her life. "For a moment, I considered sneaking into Padraig's home and slitting his throat when he returned from the shed, but I couldn't shake off this gnawing question in the back of my mind: why wasn't Emmanuel able to get away with it? Padraig's shed has no windows."

Malena swirls her finger through the air rapidly. "So, I looked around for security cameras, but all I saw were a pair of red lights dancing in sync, peering at me from behind the dark blue truck in the driveway, and a hawk in the sky above it. Looking deeper into the darkness of the brush, I noticed at least three other pairs, and I knew immediately that the ones that attacked us weren't the only demons he had built, and that some must be guarding his home. Those probably alerted him as soon as Emmanuel made it onto his land."

Silvia ponders the information as they stop at a red light, tapping the steering wheel absentmindedly. "So, he has an automated security system that can kill us on the spot?"

"Yes. And, I wish that were all..." Malena ominously interjects. "Once I saw it was futile to try and stop Padraig at his own home, I left and followed the city lights and gravel road leading from that Devil's house, hoping it would lead to Chula Vista and your church. Around sunrise, the green car that was sitting in Padraig's driveway drove past me, and the boy from the window was in the back seat, but Padraig was nowhere to be seen. In fact, there was no one driving the car at all; it must be another one of his monsters. So, there's no telling how many or what kind of other creations are inside as well."

"Are you sure about that? It was a green car driving itself. Did it look fancy or luxurious?" Silvia asks calmly, yet abruptly.

Why is she clinging to that detail? Malena wonders with a skeptical gaze, hidden only by her shades. "No, not at all. It was as plain as any car you could have ever found in Dos Ojos."

Silvia takes a deep breath and grips the steering wheel tightly. "It sounds like the boy you saw is one of our students. Between the hair and the car, it's almost impossible to believe it could be anyone other than Rian Singer." She surmises.

"Wait, you know ese hijo de puta? That's great! We can just go to the police, report his father, and we'll be able to save Emmanuel."

Suddenly, Malena's seat belt tightens around her chest, preventing her from flinging forward through the windshield as the tires of Silvia's car scream. Malena's sunglasses slide to the tip of her nose, but are stopped as she reaches to shield her face out of instinct. Silvia's car now sits, dead still, in the road. "¿Qué pasa, Silvia? ¿Qué demonios?" Malena shouts at the normally collected Silvia.

"Malena. Please, don't ever speak of any of the children of Armonia in that way again. Rian has done nothing to earn your disrespect. He's a sweet boy, who told the entire class, on his first day of school, that his dream was to use technology to create a peaceful, happy world." Silvia takes in a calming breath that upon release seems to take all her anger with it. "Nesho has been obsessed with that pure-hearted kid since that declaration, and Nesho is never wrong when it comes to people's hearts."

"Now, let's redirect that anger and disrespect to Rian's supposed father." Silvia warns, allowing the car to come back to a roll, before hitting the accelerator once more and restarting the journey to the unnamed doctor.

No fue para tanto. Casi me mataste, bruja fría. "Sorry, sorry. You're right." Malena rushes to calm her friend. She had seen her annoyed before, but anger was something new. "Anyway, can't we go to the police? We can do that first and visit your doctor later." She suggests.

Silvia seems to ponder the plan for a moment, but Malena is certain she is merely finding a way to shoot down her too-easy-to-work plan. "There are a few issues with that. One, Padraig isn't listed as the legal parent or guardian of Rian Singer. His mother, Tatiana Singer registered him into the program earlier this past August, listing his father's name as Patrick. He was apparently homeschooled before then, and, based on his testing results, they did a solid job."

"Okay, so the names don't exactly match up. Why couldn't we go to the police? Malena questions, confused.

"Well, because even though his name was fake, I'm sure his money and connections are real. On Rian's first day, his father made him ride to school alone in that car you described. Given there's no tint on the windows, it's something that I'm certain would turn a cop's head as it did to everyone at the school when it drove away by itself. It would have been a bigger fuss among the staff too if he didn't also have Rian bring a check and hand it to his homeroom teacher like it was a note telling her he'd be leaving early for the dentist." Silvia pauses, considering the power that must accompany such wealth. "Malena, that check was a donation that could fund Armonia School for five years, our entire k-12 program; the memo just said, 'The Abeona will pick Rian up every day at 3:00.'"

Malena leans back in her seat and sighs. *I knew it felt too good to be true.* "So, he's a rich psycho who has probably paid off the police, in the same way he paid you all off to turn a blind eye to the weird situation."

"We weren't paid off." Silvia defends. Rian seemed to be safe and happy. He's an awkward boy that has a hard time making friends, but he never once seemed like he was in danger. So, we just let it go." Silvia bites the nail on her right hand, clearly feeling an emotion that was more foreign than her smile: regret. "We couldn't have been more wrong about that, huh?" Silvia half admits with melancholic sarcasm.

Malena looks out the window, turning her gaze from the unfamiliar disposition of Silvia. "The sooner we get this chip out of me, the sooner we can come up with a real plan to both save Emmanuel and help Rian." Malena attempts to comfort, slowly raising her hand and patting Silvia's shoulder. "So, how far are we?"

"We're only a few minutes out from the doctor. Soon, you won't have to worry about being monitored. You see that building a few blocks away?" Silvia responds.

Malena sees what looks like a castle of two kings. One side a clean silver with lit glass panes from base to crown, while the other is of weathered, red-brown brick that only rose to two-thirds of the other's height. "Let me guess, your doctor is on the ugly side?"

"Good instincts. Most functions of the hospital were transferred to the new addition since construction finished on that side. The old side is mostly unused, only housing the morgue and old records until it can be renovated as well." Silvia responds, "Of course, we will be parking at the garage connected to the old building, and my friend will come down to let us in and take us to an unused room he keeps functioning for our, less-than-legal, guests."

"And why would he do that? How do you know him anyway?" Malena questions. "I feel like you should tell me a bit more about the man who'll be operating on me."

"I'll tell you all about it once all this trouble you brought to my doorstep is cleared away." Silvia says with a titter as they pass the final light between them and the parking garage. "For now, let's just say he owes me his life."

"I see. The Angel of Dos Ojos still doles out her blessings." Malena jokes. *You never change.*

Malena sits in silence for the remainder of the drive, all the way until Silvia parks in front of a door at the back of the old parking garage. A thick scent of urine wafts into the car, betraying the vagrants that must frequent the neglected cement shelter, its walls concerningly cracked and its paint marking each spot faded to nothing. *Looks like we're here.*

Silvia parks next to the only other vehicle in the garage, a cream-colored sedan, whose logo on the back is composed of the letters "D" and "S" in the shape of a swan. Before they can so much as shut the van's doors behind them, the door leading inside swings open, and a boisterous man yells from the doorway. "Silvia, there's my guardian angel."

The man's kind, booming voice causes Malena to step back. After becoming accustomed to Padraig and Silvia, its aggressive warmth was unnerving.

The man's features are as nondescript as they come. A white man with blonde hair and brown eyes, the same height as Silvia, 5'7", but sixty pounds heavier. His green scrubs seem a bit tight around his stomach, suggesting his eating habits of late had caught up with him.

"Thank you as always, Dr. Renner." Silvia greets the man, bowing her head slightly out of respect and gratitude.

"Now, now. None of that. I owe you for everything." He assures with both his hands cringing before relaxing and holding out his hand. "And you must be, the friend. What's with the sunglasses, you two? You look like celebrities avoiding the paparazzi" He jokes.

"I'm not sure Silvia wants me to say." Malena answers honestly, grasping his palm.

"Is that so? Well, that puts you in the running for my most interesting patient of the night!" Dr. Renner laughs, shaking her hand.

"Merely in the running?" Malena queries, curious if the doctor was fully aware of what this meeting entailed.

Dr. Renner gestures the two women inside, with a rushed wave and comforting smile. "I'll tell you along the way. Silvia tells me this is an emergency, so we better get started!"

Malena follows Silvia's lead as she saunters past the Doctor, into the stairwell behind him. The door slams shut at their backs with a click from the lock. "Up we go, your room will be on the third floor, so I hope today wasn't leg day for you." Dr. Renner jests with a guffaw.

"I'm sure we'll fare fine, but are you sure you'll be able to lift that belly the whole way?" Silvia pokes dryly, both a humorous jab and concern for her friend's health.

"Ouch. How are you going to make fun of the belly you created?" Dr. Renner laughs as they jog up. "All the extra work you give me leaves me with no time to cook. And how can I resist the taco truck outside?"

Silvia considers the notion with a sigh. "Well, I'll need to start bringing you some homemade tacos then. I'm sure it's healthier than whatever you are ordering."

Malena feels the core of her soul flare, like embers during a light breeze, at the exchange. *Seems like she's had good company since she left the village.* She thinks as she silently scales past the second story and on to the third flight of stairs, Dr. Renner at her back and Silvia in front of her.

As they reach the fourth flight, a nurse in baby-blue scrubs is seen waiting, nervously playing with the shimmering purple stethoscope around her neck with her right foot holding the door to the third floor ajar. "Dr. Renner, we need to get them to their room, quickly!" She says in a screaming whisper; her shoulder-length, twist-out curls bouncing as she points at the doctor with her eyes. "The officers want to know if it's possible to release *him* so they can transport him to OMDC."

OMDC? Malena wonders to herself. "¿Silvia, de qué se trata eso?" She asks, attempting to hide her ignorance with Spanish.

Silvia opens her mouth to answer, but a shout from Dr. Renner steals her attention. "What?! That boy needs a mental health evaluation and help, not a jail cell!" Dr. Renner steps in front of all three women, leading the charge.

"So, you're treating a prisoner today? Is that what's more interesting than Malena?" Silvia inquires.

"Yes and no. As you know, we treat those in custody and prisoners in this wing all the time. Keeping them as far away from regular patients, both as a precaution and to protect their dignity, is standard." He responds, his neck turning red. "But, this boy is more than just another jail case. While he is clearly mentally ill and poses a danger to himself and others, if he's placed in a holding cell, the lucid way in which he talks about his supposed crime tonight makes me wonder if he truly committed a crime at all." Dr. Renner pauses for a moment as they round a corner, making sure the way is clear. "And from what I've overheard, the police can't fully explain the situation quite yet either. I think they want to pin the situation on an easy scape…"

Malena sees an officer back out from the only room with closed curtains. "Hurry up, transport is nearly here." Following the officer, a young man shuffles out from the curtains. Handcuffs and leg restraints, linked by a chain that prevents him from lifting his arms, hug the ankles of his worn jeans and the wrists of his shirt that appears to have been ripped in a scuffle; his long, filthy hair fell like a veil of serpents on all sides of his head, covering the majority of his face. Malena can't help but scrutinize, searching for the eyes of the boy. His sunken, gray irises look back through the vines, seeming to search for nothing more than the end to what must have been a lifetime of suffering. Malena's very spirit cries for the boy.

Without warning, Malena feels herself snatched into darkness; the sudden jostling causes her sunglasses to slip from her face, allowing the boy's gray to meet her bronze. *No mames.*

WILLIAM

The two women wearing sunglasses disappear into a dark room on the opposite end of the hall from his own. The shorter Latin woman, with eyes that seemed to be filled with pity, had been yanked by her friend with the ink black hair into a room now blocked by Dr. Renner's quick approach to the officers. Nurse Niki, staying back, shuts the door behind them calmly, and picks up the fallen sunglasses before the officers can notice.

The wood on the door twists and deforms as a wrinkled, human face slowly protrudes from its leaf. The toothful, menacing smile extends to where ears would lay on a man, and its width takes up nearly half of the creature's face.

Oh Will, I hate to see you like this. The creature speaks to William, its teeth moving in the gums as its thin lips remain a still border to its maw. *You'll never be free again if they take you, you know? If you say something about the rats hiding behind this door, maybe you can distract the cops.* The creature cackles as it sinks back into the door, its leaf returned to normal. The boy flutters his index and middle fingers, creating a rapid metronome. *Then you can kill the pigs! Just like that poor, charitable woman's father.*

PRISM 2

CHAINED

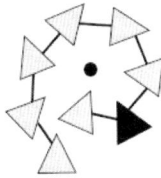

WILLIAM

William ignores the voice; his spirit too weak, and his soul exhausted. If it weren't for the restraints binding his hands and feet with loose chains, he would have silenced the creature for good. Self-immolation, to rid the world of the demon; a small recompense for the grievous crime he had committed, in a moment of fear. His only solace is that this arrest may be the only chance to explain himself and apologize to the woman that had helped him, paying her back for her kindness was now entirely out of the question. *Listening to you is why I'm here.* William responds, looking to the floor as his dry, cracked fingers continue their dance.

> **Oh, don't get accusatory with me now. You saw the man's eyes; he was black-eyed death himself. You're a hero! They just don't know it. A martyr.** The face reappears at

William's bound feet; the mask now comprised of an aged yellow skin with black speckles dotted over it unevenly. *Besides, if it were up to me, you wouldn't have been there. All I wanted was to eat stolen candy bars in our tent tonight; But no, you wanted to spend hours, searching the entire neighborhood for her car so you could deliver a pitiful thank you note for a little sandwich. Obsessive creep. Otherwise, you wouldn't have bumped into that demon.*

While unable to ignore the creature, whom he had appropriately named Peril, William had avoided falling prey to the vilest suggestions and jabs of the insidious creature for six years. It has always been clear to William, ever since the day he ran away from the only home he had ever known, that Peril was, and always will be, a relentless instigator that wants nothing more than violence and revelry in its own pleasures. A monster, to be kept far from decent society.

Don't you ignore me you scrawny, baggy-eyed creep. Peril screams at the boy, its smile momentarily flipping into a frown, before the mountain returns to the typical, deep valley that graced the monster's face. *Oh, I see. You think just because, for once, someone noticed and helped you, that you're too good for your oldest friend? That, because someone was so sad, so down on themselves, that they happened to be staring at the ground. Just long enough to notice the dung they were about to step in.* Peril guffaws, as he disappears back into the floor. *When will you learn? You are nothing.*

William feels an authoritative shove at his back, pushing him forward, past Nurse Niki and Dr. Renner. They remain to the side, Dr. Renner's skin flushing with pent up anger as Nurse Niki mutters something in his ear, holding his arm like a vice. An argument had obviously taken place. But he honestly wasn't sure what it could have been about, having been completely consumed in fighting the taunts of Peril. The second officer at his back repeatedly jostles him forward, to hurry his steps toward the elevator that brought them here earlier that night.

"I can't believe we got stuck watching this boring asshat." The officer in the front bemoans. "I was hoping he'd have an episode or two, like he did on the scene. I'm falling asleep here."

"Who you telling, Smiles?" The second officer complains. "There was a house explosion and everything going on out there, and here we are transferring this bum to OMDC."

William follows the officers without uttering a single word, the duet of clanking chains and his fluttering fingers were the music to the officers' song of petty grievance. ***See? You're even boring the cops, William! Don't you want to feel that thrill again? When you fought for your life? When you beat death itself?*** Peril prods as he reappears, undulating along the surface of the walls to follow them around the corner. ***Don't tell me you didn't love it! Listen. Just jump at him, bite his neck, and latch on for dear life. It would be so easy.*** Peril suggests, thinning its eyes.

Do it. Do it. Do it! The creature repeats, consuming William's attention once more. Each repeat birthing a new double on the wall, giving it the semblance of a museum filled with ceremonial masks. The deafening chant quickly breaks past the percussion of William's fingers.

"Shut the hell up! I'm not listening anymore." William yells, his diaphragm constricting as soon as the final word leaves his lips. The cop at his back delivers a quick fist to the back of his head, and the seventeen-year-old nearly trips. His neck jerks at the sudden shift, and his vision briefly flashes white. Nothing he hasn't experienced before.

"Now, I'll say this one more time, before this gets ugly, son." The officer warns, without a bit of care in his gruff, Texan voice. "The elevator on this side of the hospital is down, and transport is here. We're taking the stairs to level one of the parking garage so we can keep your mange and crazy away from the nice, healthy minded people of this hospital. So, get moving."

William nods in Officer Smiles' direction with complete submission, and the tall, lanky officer grunts at his quick submission. William follows the officer through the stairwell entrance to the left of the elevators, and watches as Smiles descends the first flight.

"What the hell is taking you so long?" The officer behind him berates, causing him to lean into his first step down in haste. He was certain another blow would find its way to his skull if he didn't hustle.

Unfortunately, he was right. In that very moment, William's back is met with yet another quick push from Officer Gates, and he hurls down the stairs as Peril takes form in the cement landing below, opening his jaw to meet him. The corners of his lips sharpen, and the deep valleys of his cheeks become bottomless trenches. ***You should have tasted Officer Smiles when you had the chance.*** The monster mocks, as William plummets past Officers Smiles, and into Peril's waiting gullet.

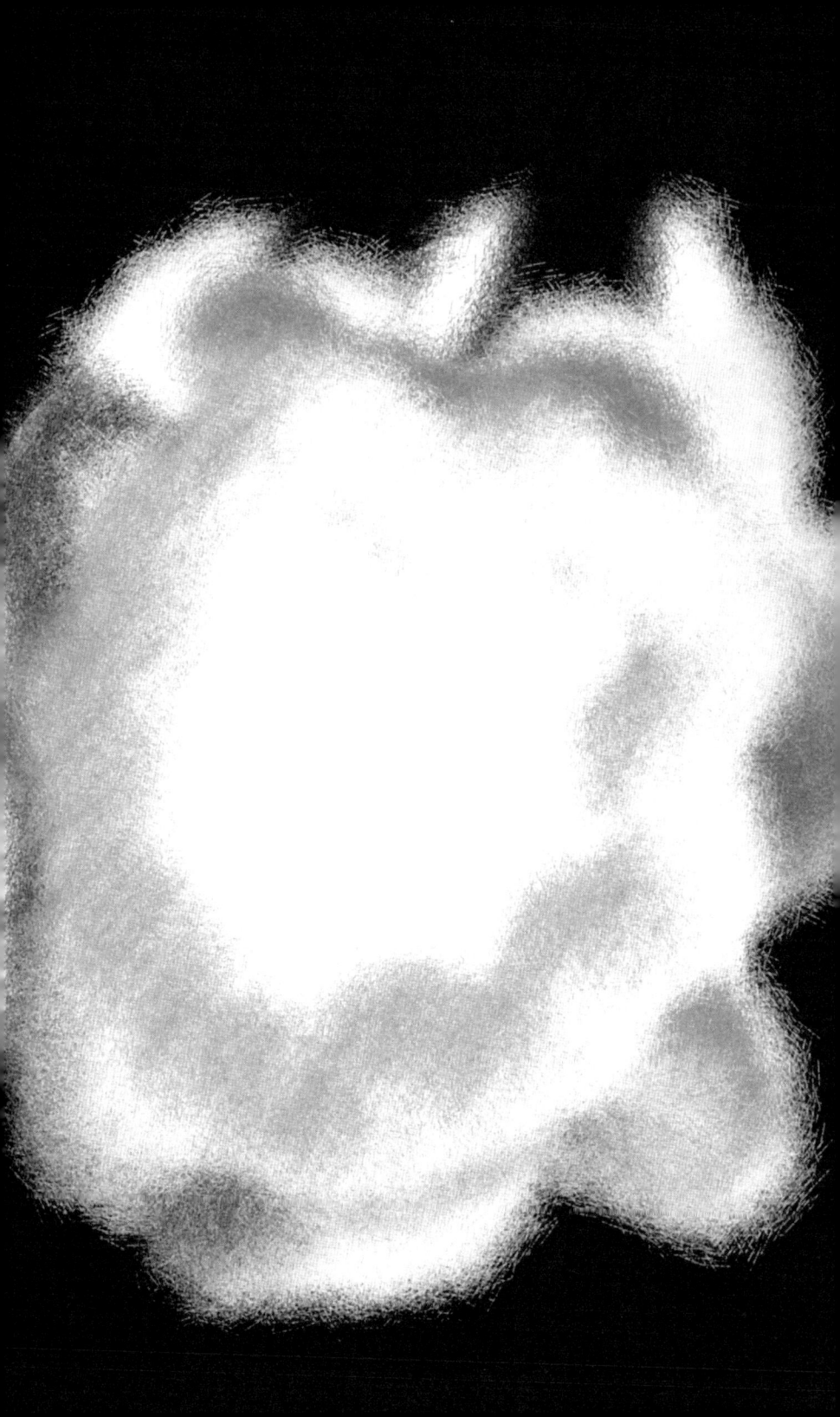

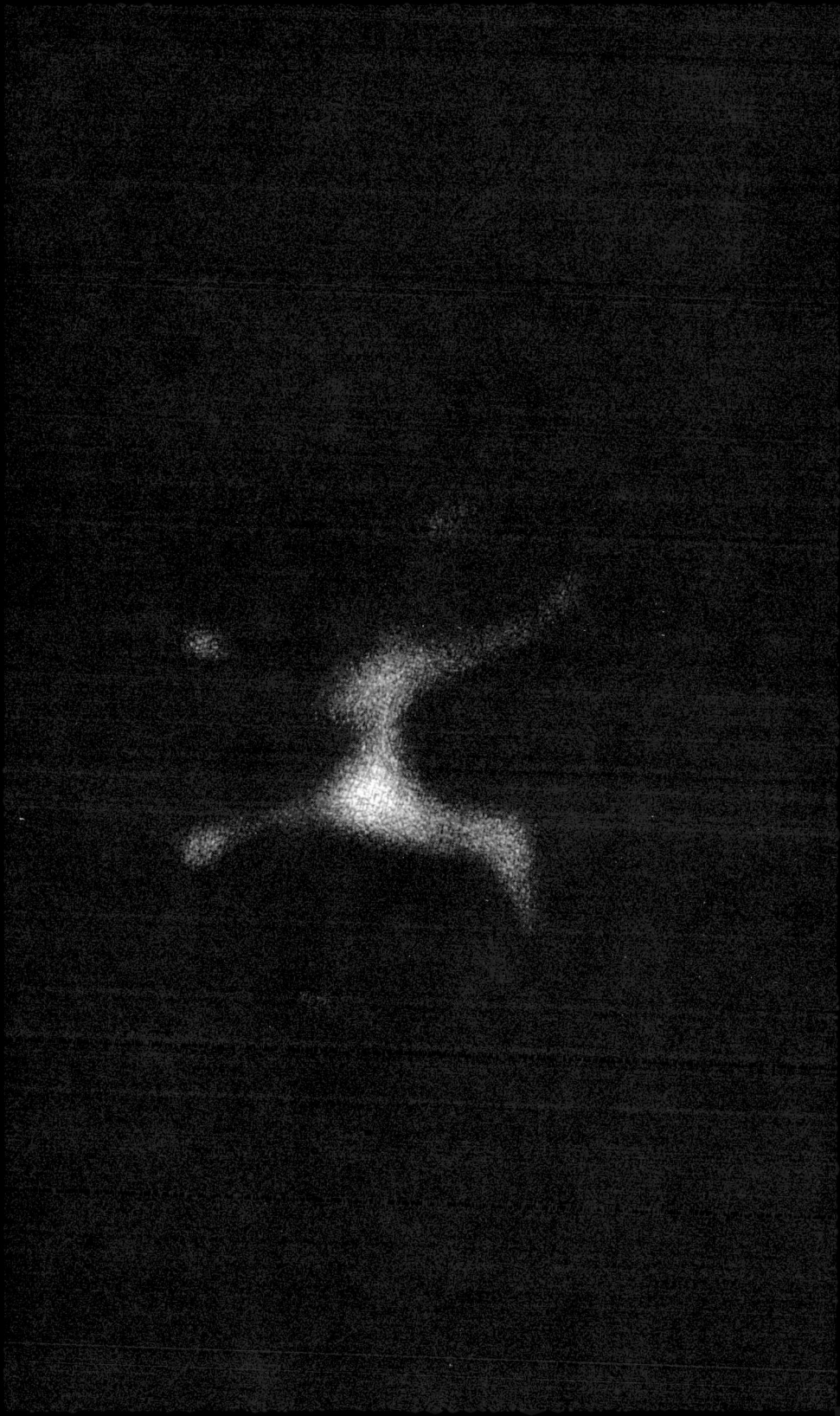

["Now."]

The eyes of the one known as William slowly open up to a sterile room filled with two long silver tables to his right, and surgical tools and a wall length desk on his left. A young doctor with dark brunette hair, wearing dark blue scrubs, combs his fingers through his goatee in thought while sitting in front of the computer at the far end of the desk near the door.

"Well, I guess I can't complain. At least it wasn't a boring night." He concludes to himself as he records his notes, a sure ending to a conversation he was holding with himself to stay awake.

Wasting no time, The Sombra stands, silently placing himself behind the unaware forensic pathologist.

["Blunt force trauma due to fall in the stairwell. Skull fractures and several bruises on the hands, knees, ankles and knees."] The Sombra reads aloud, commenting on the circumstance of its birth. The doctor starts to pivot his chair, but is met with a surgical knife in his temple. ["How tragic. He truly believed his own demons had engulfed him in his final hour."] The murderer declares without a tinge of regret as he bends the doctor's head over the back of the chair and snaps his neck by pressing his body weight onto it as he twists the doctor's skull.

The Sombra removes the doctor's clothing, and places him where William's body once laid lifeless. He unsheathes the blade and taps his head with the dripping surgical blade. The youthful doctor's face is twisted in terror, and blood spills from the wound in his temple, pooling around the floor drain at the feet of William's naked body, now ruled by The Sombra.

I guess the next step is to cut these filthy locks and get dressed. The Sombra thinks as he heads over to the array of bladed surgical tools, selecting a set of black-handled scissors. He stands above the corpse that would never rise again, and removes the onyx hair caked in mud and moss. *Sorry Doc, it was nothing personal, but I have to think of my own survival. I can't have you blabbing to everyone you know about how your patient became a 'zombie' with black hair.*

I could just kiss you! Finally, some beautiful action. The voice of Peril sings, taking shape in the scarlet waterfall cascading off the edge of the table, ignoring its flow.

The Sombra stares down at the dripping mask, bewildered, but unflinching as he continues snipping away his former identity. ["That is unexpected. I assumed this brain was healed along with the body, but this disease is still present."]

I'm no disease, you glorified chauffeur. I am the very will of this body you've stolen; Will's natural state and now, lucky you, your new boss! The voice of Peril says in a self-confident, irreverent tone.

["I am no child, Peril. I am the culmination of over a thousand lifetimes, many much worse than an insistent and self-destructive hallucination. Feel free to watch as I carry out that boy's final wish."] The Sombra offers his unwanted guest, as he seesaws the scissors through the final, thickest lock.

Peril scoffs as the anaconda like mass of hair falls onto the forensic pathologist. **You think you're worth any more than that boy? That you can accomplish anything worthwhile,**

where he couldn't? Peril's face extends beyond the bloody flow and snakes through the air to meet The Sombra's face. ***Dead or alive, you'll end up just like that good-for-nothing, trite man-child. An innocuous failure, a worthless crumb eater. You'll be zilch to the world, including that Thela you want to help so badly.***

The Sombra taps his new fingers on his chin. *Zilch. I like that. It reminds me of home.* He considers, thrusting Peril to the back of his mind as he brushes his shoulders free of stray hairs. *Rest easy William, your spirit is now my own and I, Zilch, will pay your debt to Thela.*

Zilch quickly dresses himself in the dark blue scrubs, pinning the doctor's badge on the breast pocket. Glancing back at the desk for anything that could be useful, he notices an inch-long black strip that trails underneath. The curious belt of nylon leads Zilch to a convenient discovery, a black backpack with yellow trimming along its borders. He throws the bag over his shoulder, leaving the morgue behind.

On the way to the old parking garage, he passes by a bathroom and decides to check his handiwork. *Not bad for blind and freehand.* He thinks, admiring his makeover to William's body. Gone are the vines, replaced with spiky, pure obsidian grass; the hairs on top no longer than his index finger, and those at the back fell no further than the nape of his neck. A gleam of cold light betrays the new brillo, dormant within the darkness. *Soon my child. We'll find you a home soon enough, but we have work to do first.*

What was once William's emaciated, nearly six-foot form, is now slim and athletic after the resurrection. The pilfered scrubs fit tightly around his chest, and the pants barely reach his ankles. The pristine, white slip-on shoes are about a half-size too tight, but they'll do.

Making full use of the respite, Zilch fishes through the junky backpack to find a silver-linked watch, a wallet, a loaded handgun, a phone, car keys, and a yellow windbreaker.

Poor guy. He must have been worried, being all alone on this side of the hospital and surrounded by nothing but prisoners, and dead bodies. Peril chimes, his face poking into the peripheral of Zilch. ***I bet he never would have guessed that someone who was both would do him in!*** The evil mask laughs with elation.

Zilch feels a tinge of regret for the life lost, but no more than a man who shoots a feral, rabid dog to avoid a bite from the diseased beast. *If a witness to the revival can't be convinced that what they saw was a misunderstanding or that their mind was playing tricks, there is only one recourse for a sombra: to eliminate the threat.* He surmises, clicking the watch onto his left wrist. *Ahh, 8:30am. I'll be cutting it close, but I should make it. Even if I have to walk.*

Zilch throws on the yellow jacket, and places the gun in the waistband of his scrubs, while the surgical knife he used to kill the pathologist is thrown into the right pocket of the jacket.

Zilch leaves the bathroom and heads straight for the first level of the old parking garage. Not a soul was present amongst the weathered columns; no cops and no cars. *The Davy-Swan must have belonged to Dr. Renner.* He considers, completely fine with walking to his destination; turning back and retrieving the vehicle from the newer garage would have put him in contact with too many witnesses to his exit.

In fact, part of Zilch looks forward to the calm before the initiation of his plan, but Peril stubbornly makes such a notion impossible.

Just steal it! He's not even watching his own backpack. He's probably too hungry and weak to stop you. They steal from each other all the time!

I have all that I need to make my plan work. I'll leave him to his begging.

You're just going to let this child dance on my face. Kick the little bastard's knees out!

Don't put yourself on the sidewalk, and you won't have to worry about him. Zilch retorts, his irritation growing.

With every passerby and store front, crimes are suggested, indulgence is encouraged, and violence is demanded.

Oh look, Mocha Mocha! We should stop by and gorge on their steaming, fresh croissants. At the end of the day the owner, Momo, hands out any leftovers to pathetic souls like William; they were always his favorite. Something we actually agreed on. Peril asserts as the letters on a street sign rearrange into his form. **Don't you want to taste something for yourself? For the first time? We could grab a coffee too!**

Tasting with my own tongue would be nice, but I have no need to eat, and William's true desire comes first. If we're late by even a minute, we'll lose our chance.

Zilch tries to maintain his calm but the comments and ceaseless prodding rip him away from his own thoughts at every moment. What would have been his first walk under a clear sky and blissful sun, sullied. The faces, blipping away and reforming on a new surface at a whim, overshadow the favorable weather and light breeze with unpredictable and unbearable pleas.

This is what William lived with every moment of his life? Zilch questions, knowing very well the answer. Even with every minute memory that filled William's head, this experience is far worse than The Sombra could have predicted. As a brillo takes over the body, every facet of its host is healed and renewed. The body is rebuilt into its ideal state; organs, nerves, and muscle alike are healed, but this process does not account for a brain that was flawed from the beginning.

Ignoring the demon only makes the symptoms worse. The faces multiply on the sand-colored walls of the apartment buildings and the voices begin to echo in unison. Though he avoids the eyes of others as he walks down the palm-tree lined sidewalks of East Palomar Street, he can see the lower portions of their face begin to morph into the signature derisive gleam. **What's wrong? The big bad doppelganger too shy to look strangers in their face?** Peril chides.

Only halfway through his trek, The Sombra pauses for a moment in Heritage Park, seeking the peace William felt as he watched the ducks or geese paddling away in the water. *I just need to make it to the library. He's not real. Center yourself, Zilch.* But instead, as he reaches the edge of the small pond and peers down the slope, he is greeted with the familiar, evil mask. The entire pond surface was now Peril.

Poor Zilch. Even after a thousand lifetimes, a human body is still a human body. A slave to its brain, making you just like anyone else. A slave to your inner callings; to temptations dark and innocent alike. A slave to me. My dear old William avoided his darkest desires for six years by satiating me with minor favors; how long do you think you'll last if you ignore me completely?

["Your wants were never William's. William desired such things."] Zilch yells, both out of fear and indignance. ["He was a peaceful young man, doing his best to protect the world from your poison! Even in his dying moments, all he wished for was to pay back the kindness Thela showed him. To offer her something in return for the pain he caused her."]

Peril laughs as a tickle rises up Zilch's leg and he looks down to find his foot crushing an anthill. Masks no bigger than sesame seeds erupt from the opening and climb up his leg using prehensile teeth to scurry forward. Zilch jumps back and slaps away at the army of Peril in a panic, knocking them off like a deranged King Kong on the tower.

Once the miniature army is thwarted, Zilch stiffens as he notices joggers and dog walkers pausing to assess the strange man yelling in the park. *Shit.* He thinks as he hurries to escape the scene.

Now that is funny. You're already cracking! Peril mocks as Zilch begins to jog in desperation toward the library. **The indomitable sombra, a physically perfect being with no need to eat, can't handle William's world. You finally get your chance to enjoy life, but here you are, fragile and vulnerable.**

And Peril is right. While sombras are unaging and immortal, they are not invulnerable as William himself had proven. And for that very reason, for the fact that Zilch had experienced death a thousand times yet true life and agency for only an hour, he can't ignore the demonic, mental artifact that plagues him. The idea that he wasn't in control, and may never be in control, spirals and creates the perfect storm for Peril.

The clouds themselves morph into the visage, some smiling and some frowning in disapproval. The voices become disjointed as the clouds sporting grins encourage the quickening dash with a derisive tone, and the scowls clamor for him to either stab any of the random pedestrians he passes, or trip and die himself. Only William's inherited final wish and the sombra's instinctive goal to fulfill it drives Zilch forward and keeps the madness at bay.

The open mouth of a sidewalk Peril protrudes from the cement and nips at the air under his foot, causing him to trip. Barely catching his face, Zilch curses the new sense of fear that had momentarily conquered him. *What am I doing?* He chastises as he stands up, and glances at his watch. *Ten more minutes,*

Peril. Once I make it, I'll be on the road to achieving William's wish to repay Thela and being free of you. Zilch proclaims with false certainty.

You really think it will be that easy, don't you? That Padraig will set that bastardized corpse free and take the time away from pursuing his own goals to fix your twisted mind? And all for some information on the front end and the promise of your aid once he's done, huh? A single Peril questions from the sky as the others fade away. **Go ahead, I'd love to see you try. Like a dog pulling on his master's leash.** Peril disappears from the sky with a jeering laugh, as Zilch restarts his step, and heads toward West Chula Vista Library.

Each peaceful step leaves the sombra leery of the mask's return, but the clouds remain clouds and the signs maintain their letters and numbers all the way up to the steps of West Chula Vista. Zilch rests on the sandy-white staircase, counting down the final two minutes until his ride arrives as he admires the sun in the sky. ["Such a beautiful day. I hope Abeona arrives soon."] He mumbles to himself.

As if the heavens felt inclined to answer his prayers early, Zilch watches her pull into the street parking that lines the sidewalk of the library, directly in front of the plotting sombra. Out pops Rian, an unceremonious grin painted on his face as he steps out. The wind whisks his red hair to the side as he searches for Nesho with his hand on his forehead to block the sun.

Time to start the show. Zilch thinks, covertly grabbing the blade of the surgical knife. Tunnel vision ensues as he slowly approaches Rian from the side, as if he were going to cross the street.

Just feet away, Rian waves. A friendly greeting to a stranger perhaps? Zilch could care less, as he brings up his knife, halting the wave midair. ["Don't make any sudden movements. Get back in the car and take me to see your father."] He commands. Rian raises his hands as his smile melts to a fearful frown and obliges as he starts to back up into the open door of the vehicle.

Then, as he looks past Zilch, Rian's mouth shoots open with a gasp. From behind, a hand snatches the collar of Zilch's jacket, attempting to pull him in the opposite direction. He swivels his head to see, none other than, the face of Peril. Now with a body dawned in a platinum hoodie, the creature brandishes its derisive smile as its teeth move to speak. ***Whoa there boy, you almost pulled free.*** He laughs. ***Looks like you'll need some obedience training. I can't stand a dog that pulls on his leash.***

Zilch twists his body around madly, the loose collar threatening to strangle him as he swings the blade across Peril's visage.

With the death-dealing swipe of the knife, Zilch sails through the right eye of the antagonistic mask. But the hallucination vanishes, and Zilch finds himself staring, in disbelief, into the remaining, hickory left eye, of Nesho White.

NESHO WHITE

Blood from his sliced open eye spews into the air, following the trajectory of the blade. The cut, inches deep, destroyed Nesho's right eye and sliced into the bridge of his nose. It all happened so fast. Moments earlier he was sitting near the top of the steps, on the bench just outside the library door. He skipped down the steps upon seeing the Abeona in the distance, but then he noticed a strange man he'd never seen before, sneaking something out from his pocket and looking at Rian. Nesho's instincts told him to stop the strange man, so he followed as the man approached, jumping from the stairs to pull his collar back. But then, the moment he touched the ground, the vision in his right eye went black as blood flew through the air in front of the other.

He's going to kill me, Nesho thinks as the adrenaline permeating his being prevents the recognition of pain. *But at least Rian can get away.* "Rian! Ru..." He starts to yell as a metal barrel is pulled out from the carjacker's waistband and placed in front of his left eye.

["Damn you, Peril! Look what you've done!"] The stranger berates as he slowly pulls the trigger. ["When you wake up, come find me."] Is all Nesho hears as a flash in the barrel flares. Nesho feels the puncture of his other eye, as it explodes like a water balloon poked by a needle. His vision nonexistent, the last thing he hears before his thoughts fade is a distant scream from the voice of his dear Silvie: "Nesho! No!"

He never even feels his body hit the ground. He is merely surrounded by an all-encompassing darkness, matched only by the shooter's abysmal eyes, as his thoughts die out.

PRISM 1: PART 1

ENCORE

NESHO WHITE

Death is inevitable for all living creatures. Those fortunate enough, will never fully understand their own existence to begin with; the unfortunate do not share in this ignorance. For the ignorant, death is merely the eternal cessation of all function, allowing the body's nutrients to be returned to the planet that gave it life. For the sentient, of which humans currently make up the vast majority, death is a sorrowful affair.

All sentient beings will undergo The Final Dream upon the death of their mind or body; a dream not of the mind, but of a creature's entire self. A dream that falls over the mind, body, spirit, and soul. It is not felt or seen, but experienced in a way that is impossible for a mind of the lower plane to comprehend.

For some, it is an epic battle in an unending war that finally comes to a crushing defeat, for others it's a simple dinner at home where the bellies of the family are full and all parties leave the table. In all cases, one member is left at the scene on their own, wishing the dream could continue. A swordsman standing against his foe, wishing to fight another day. A home cook, wishing to share another meal. The death of Nesho White, is no different.

The dream opens with Nesho sitting upon the stage, wearing a full, azure suit with his signature platinum hoodie draped over his shoulders like a cape, the sleeves wrapped around his neck like an ascot. His curls are pulled back into a simple bun, save for a few stray curls falling over his face and swaying in front of his eyes like the pendulum of a grandfather clock as a birling blizzard of Antonio Vivaldi's *Winter* is skillfully rendered upon the strings of his pristine, maple violin. The flurry of snow and ice is nearly palpable, pelting the audience with terrifying wonder.

Only the two spotlights illuminating the heart of the storm provide any respite. One for the curly-haired musician, and the other for a dancer in a silver and black, sleeveless unitard. Her long and flowing hair, like silk, umber curtains, obscures her face with every twist. On the far side, hidden in the shadows of stage left, stands a proud stage manager, nodding his head in glowing approval and struggling not to applaud.

All three appear nothing less than gratified as Nesho's bow strokes come to an end and the final note guides the last snowy gust through the auditorium.

The house lights come on, revealing the full glory of the auditorium and the crowd in the seats. They quickly rise from their golden-legged, shimmering periwinkle seats, cheering for the grand performance. The stage manager jogs to the front of the platinum-colored stage and grabs the dancers' hand, bowing to the fevered cheers. Nesho remains seated, placing his violin down as he takes in the scene. His eyes are loving and accepting; they are full and satisfied.

Soon, the applause dies down and the patrons begin to file out through the Aegean blue doors lining the back walls. The stage manager and the dancer, together, jump down from the stage, and onto one of the long carpets that match the deep blue exits. They meander along the path toward the doors, savoring the end of their performance.

I approach Nesho from his right, offering a chance at the big time. ["That was quite the show. Shame that it's over."] I say to the seated musician, but he simply looks back to me and smiles. ["Wouldn't you like to play again? As it so happens, I have another show that could use your talents, though you would have to leave your old instrument behind."] I offer, bringing his attention to the violin, darker than the shadows themselves, that I held by its neck. I pull out a large, crystalline book and open it on his music stand, tossing aside his own. ["This book contains all the music I've managed to gather from across the world.

Every song I've ever heard, from songs you never knew existed to even the concertos in your flimsy, old book, can be found in these pages. Why don't you try out the first one using this new violin? Just one song, and I bet you'll never want to put it down."]

"No, I'm okay." The boy declares, with a toothy smile. "The show is over. I practiced my entire life for this moment, and now that it's over, I'm done. I played my best, and I have no regrets. It was a great performance!"

["But it was so short. You didn't enjoy playing?"] I ask, knowing the inky-black aura of the violin should have tempted the musician beyond comprehension; like a peach stolen from the orchard of the Gods with its enthralling and addictive scent.

"Of course, I did." The youth declares, arching one eyebrow at my question.

["Well, my show is indefinite. It will never end, and you can forever be a part of it. The only requirement is that you match the rest of our group and use the black violin."] I inch the violin closer to him, but he pushes it back gently as he shakes his head in refute.

"That sounds a bit tedious." Nesho retorts, scrunching his face for a moment before switching to a pitying smile. "All good things come to an end. That's why they're so enjoyable. Now it's time for me to move on to something else." The genuine joy in his voice, out of place in the bleakness of the end. I look over to see the stage director and the dancer embracing, standing just in front of the exit.

["Move on to something else? Why do that if you could do what you wanted forever?"] I ask, feeling my own end approaching at his continued rejection.

"Well, Silvie always taught me to be satisfied with what I have at the end of each day, as long as I've tried my best. And though I found schoolwork to be a bore, every day I lived to improve myself, diving into the wonders of the world and learning new skills so I could help others like my mom or Silvie do." Nesho stiffens up from embarrassment, realizing he was carrying on with a complete stranger. "Sorry about that. Silvie really knocked those lessons into my head, huh?" He laughs.

Then, as the stage director holds the door open, and the dancer walks through, a forlorn, angelic voice screams from the orchestra seats. "Nesho! Play just one more song on the violin. One more, just for me. Please!" The plea grabs the boy's attention, and he smiles with the untainted elation of a child. He turns his attention to see one remaining member of the audience, and nods his head at the raven-haired owner, picking up his violin. Nesho's love fills his entirety, flowing from his heart to his fingertips. I can feel it sparking his spirit anew.

Nesho turns to the first page of the crystalline book, not allowing the surprise of the strangely organized music to throw him off; each bar of music is numbered and has its notes contained in a two-dimensional prism.

Nesho places the violin on his left shoulder and gently supports it with his chin. And, with the melodic strings nestled in place, he raises his bow to start the first song at the behest of the only remaining audience member; the woman whose voice could reach the spirit of any man, and the angel that was no less responsible for his upbringing than his own mother.

As the stage director exits the auditorium, I watch as the door swings itself shut behind him. A swing so slow, time appeared to be frozen. As if awaiting the birth of this new song; Nesho's *Spring*.

As the door nearly shuts completely, Nesho plays the first sorrowful, resonant note. As the note pierces the silence, a hand shoots out from the light of the exit. It grabs the door, holding it ajar momentarily, before throwing it wide open.

In runs the dancer, her curtain of hair billowing behind her, and the stage director at her side. They scramble across the lapis carpet to return to the stage as Nesho reaches the second prism. They leap onto the stage just as Nesho reaches the fifth, the tune transforming into one of hope and triumph.

I step to the side and take my place on the outskirts of the stage. Relegated once more to the role of observer, I watch the musician's eyes take on the color of the crystalline book as he becomes more entranced by the music with each stroke of the bow.

I am unsure what is occurring to the boy, but I am certain this outcome is not purely his own doing. ["That voice of yours truly can rouse the spirit, Silvia."]. With my defeat at the hands of Dara Lucero's offspring, there is nothing left to do except watch the youth's new performance. For now.

["Well then, show me, Nesho. Whether a human mind can handle all these memories; all of these lives."] I mutter. The stage director, revealed in the light to bear Nesho's face, grabs my book from the music stand just as the musician finishes the seventh prism. The stage director looks into the book, and I am forced back into my slumber. ["I'll be watching. From now, until your very last breath; your life, my dreams."]

Like thawing ice, warmth returns and his limbs tingle painfully as Nesho tries to move them. He tastes the metallic fog in the air as he lays on what feels like a waterbed, squishing and giving way to his every motion. As he opens his eyes, he is nearly blinded by the shine emitted from thousands of prismatic columns rising from the gelatinous floor in spiral formation, with Nesho at its center. The height of each column varies with seemingly no rhyme or reason, the shortest no more than ten feet, while the average is around thirty by Nesho's estimates. Each rectangular side of the prisms is about four feet wide, with two of the three sides housing a single glassy rod that connects each column to the one behind and in front of it. Only the shortest column, the one closest to the boy, lacks a second rod and column to connect with. The boy stands, bumping his head into a strange, obsidian glass orb that had been hovering above him. The otherworldly orb, so black it appears to be a hole in space, sits unwavering despite the agitation.

Rubbing his head, Nesho apologizes to the orb before turning back to the dwarf column and touching its smooth, glassy side, only to be gifted with the vision of his eye being slashed and the other being shot; his death plays before him with every detail and pain accounted for. Nesho pulls his hand back in shock; the experience is so visceral he can only believe it to be a memory.

"I guess that wasn't a dream." Nesho surmises, sweat forming on his brow while he tries to calm his racing heart. He looks to the other prisms closest to himself. His temptation gets

225

the best of him, and he places his hand on the second column. This time, the vision of William's death and Zilch's birth flash before him. Nesho sees the cursed mask of Peril haunting them both, and empathizes with not only William, but the opportunistic Zilch that claimed his body. "At least it wasn't on purpose." He solemnly jokes to himself with a weak chuckle, palpating his right eye.

"He probably wanted me to find him because he assumed I would turn into a sombra like himself. But, I still feel like me." Nesho guesses, playing with one of his curls in the cold light of the prism. "This light is so weird. It's like ice." The young man observes, turning his attention to the black sky and cupping his hands around his lips. "Where the hell am I?" The boy yells into the abyss surrounding the spiral maze of crystal columns. His voice merely gets lost in the void.

Unwilling to give up though, Nesho hopes the answers to his location are in the other prisms. At just a glance, the third column feels familiar, and upon his touch the memories flood into him freely. Too freely. Nesho pulls back at the tribulations of his dear Silvie and her friend Malena, the revelations nearly too outlandish for him to accept. *There's no way Rian's father could be that way when his son is so pure.* The boy thinks, but the previous memories were no lie, so he accepts these to be truths as well and places his hand back onto the column. This time he learns exactly what Zilch is, and how Silvie's own mother was one of those eternal beings.

Though shaking from the revelations of Silvie's past, Nesho continues onward, touching four more columns. Each one answering its own questions, each one just a piece of the puzzle waiting to be completed. It is only once he reaches the seventh that the boy understands all that led up to that moment, and tears stream down his face. *Oh Rian.* The boy pities, as the sky opens to reveal Silvie's cross hanging in the sky. Following the slender chain of her golden cross, he can see his second mother crying from above.

For a moment, he considers looking away and touching the alluring eighth prism of the maze, curious as to what memories it may hold. It stands tall above the rest, piercing the circle of darkness that frames the outside world and Silvie's cross. *That one must contain the memories of Silvie's mom.* Nesho assumes. In any other instance, the prism would win his attention with little competition, but his normally insatiable curiosity is no match for Silvie's begging stare. *But I'll have to save that for another day.*

As Nesho's vision focuses on her, he finds himself back in her lap, still on the sidewalk and surrounded by what must have been his own blood, if the stains on his left shoulder were any indication. Screams can be heard all around them while people are seen running from the general direction of the gunshot that had occurred seconds before, and Nesho sees the tail of the Abeona drive out of sight.

As he turns his attention back to her, Silvie stares back hesitantly, waiting to see what had become of the boy she had helped to raise. "What's wrong Silvie? Do I have something on my face?" Nesho laughs.

Suddenly, Silvie hugs Nesho as tightly as she can, praising God that he was alive; that he hadn't come back a sombra. "You're alright, thank The Lord you're alright." Silvie shouts as the streams on her cheeks wet his own. "But what happened, Nesho? What happened to your eyes?

Nesho pats Silvie on the back, comforting his other mother. "I know you have a lot of questions, Silvie, but we have to hurry and get out of here before anyone realizes." he says, nudging her to stand and giving her a comforting smile. "If we are going to put an end to Padraig's maniacal schemes and stop that sombra, Zilch, from hurting anyone else, we have to find Malena and leave now."

Silvie's eyes open wide, knowing something deeper than healed vision had occurred within the teen, but she nods back in understanding, returning his smile. Both stand to run from the scene, and, in the reflection of one of the cars, Nesho notices his eyes are now a shimmering, crystal blue; green rays seem to swim amongst the sea as well, lending it the appearance of northern lights.

What am I now? The boy wonders as he and Silvie dash toward an alley to escape the sight of any potential witnesses.

PRISM 1: PART 2

APPLE JUICE

NESHO WHITE

"Breaking News: a shocking update, and connection, on two of our earlier stories. You may remember the seventeen-year-old suspect of a double homicide, who passed away in police custody after receiving treatment at Sunset Hills Medical Campus." The radio host's rehearsed and gossipy voice narrates. A grim reminder of what lay ahead if Nesho's plan failed.

"Just hours after the teen's death, the forensic pathologist investigating his case was found dead, and his belongings stolen. Even stranger, the body of the original suspect is now missing as well. The police do have a suspect, thanks to tips from eyewitnesses and surveillance cameras – a young, white male, about 5'11" with medium length, spiked black hair. Now, are you ready for this? He was last seen during the shooting at West Chula Vista Library that we reported on earlier today, where a green sedan appears to have been stolen with a waiting teenager in the back…"

The radio is shut off, and silence takes over the tangerine cab as it pulls off the loose gravel road and onto the extensive paved driveway of the lonely, sand-colored house in the wilderness of Otay Mesa. Only the nervous tap of fingers colliding against jeans kept the car from entering complete muteness.

"Are you sure we can do this, Nesho?" Malena asks, staring out her window and into the setting sun as if it may be her last chance to witness the life-giving star. Her oddly placid tone suggests she would accept whatever answer she was given, though her fingers continue to tap away like a maddened metronome.

"We've done all we can in the past seven and a half hours. If we took any longer, Padraig and Zilch would make their move first and it would be too late for us. Taking the initiative is our only chance." Nesho responds, repeatedly unfurling and folding the screen of the rugged flip phone he had modified only a couple hours before. "The man, well, the sombra that attacked me took six hours to revive after William's fall, and two more to reach Rian so he could use the Abeona to strike a deal with Padraig. They would have expected the same of me, since my death was also violent."

During the drive back to Armonia Church, after Silvie and Nesho had snuck away from the scene, Silvie explained that she and Malena had staked out the hospital after her procedure and tailed Zilch once he exited. He was easy to spot, and it was only Malena's insistence on following him that placed Silvie at the scene of Nesho's death and resurrection.

Silvie's guilt was palpable as she blamed herself for pulling Malena and causing her glasses to slide off, putting Nesho's life in jeopardy. Still, though Silvie was grateful that the baby she had watched grow into a middle schooler was alive, she pressed him about the details of his revival.

Unfortunately, try as he might to come up with a feasible explanation, Nesho was unsure of why his revival was so quick in comparison to William's body, or why he hadn't become a sombra himself. With no time to ruminate, he chalked it up to his impatient spirit and focused his energy on creating a strategy to take down Padraig.

Eight hours was all they had to plan and prepare before Padraig would have made his move at the advice of Zilch, who would have informed Padraig about everything that had transpired between the time of Malena's kidnapping and his arrival with Rian. Nesho was certain that Padraig would never turn down the opportunity for an intellectually equal ally, even if it came at a cost. Yet, even if Zilch arrived with inhuman black eyes and hair to match, with knowledge of everything Padraig had ever done up until one day prior, Padraig was a cautious man that would require proof of Zilch's claims. Especially for the power of resurrection. If eight hours had transpired with no word or sight of the second sombra-to-come, he would have sent Latona to find and collect the body.

Malena scrutinizes the sky and Nesho leans forward to see the silhouette of the Hawk following them as it flies across the setting sun. Turning to the rear window, Nesho notices Padraig's Retriever Hound tailing them in the distance as well.

"Perfect, they're still following the tracker! That's a great sign!" Nesho declares, while patting Malena's left shoulder as an uncertain smile appears and fades on her face quicker than a blink.

A minute later, the cab slows to a halt, pulling in just behind the Abeona on the left side of the driveway. "Welp, looks like it's time to see if I'm as smart as everyone thinks." Nesho laughs, throwing the phone into his left pocket, pushing his door open, and stepping out of the vehicle in sync with Malena.

"Thanks for your help, Daniel. If you don't hear from us within fifteen minutes, you can head back." Nesho says, shutting his door before the cabbie can reply. He pats his right pocket as a muffled voice wishes him "good luck", and he nods to Malena as they both move to approach the black cherry door, passing Padraig's midnight blue truck.

"I guess we should just knock, huh?" Nesho suggests to the stoic Malena as he starts drumming a beat onto the thick leaf.

Without warning, the door swings open, and they are both greeted by the cinnamon smile of Latona, Rian's bionic caretaker; his assumed mother known as Tatiana Singer, whenever she is forced to leave the house.

Latona bows slightly, stepping to the side and gesturing inside. "Ahh, Mr. White, we're ecstatic to see you've arrived just on time." Her celeste, Penrose triangle irises dart to scan Malena, though her smile remains. "And Malena, how great to see you again, but your meeting with Master Padraig isn't until Monday morning. You still have a chance to..."

"Actually, she's my guest tonight. A show of good faith toward a future partner." Nesho interjects, stepping inside as Malena follows.

"I see. I will alert Master Padraig and Mr. Zilch that you have arrived." Latona states, shutting the door before her body stiffens as the whites of her eyes turn black. A thin, violet sliver appears, extending from the center of her tri-cornered iris. Immediately it begins to revolve like the hand of a clock, taking on the hue of its other brethren of the spectrum: indigo, blue, green, yellow, orange, red, and back to violet. The cycle continues until Latona's body relaxes ten seconds later, and the whites return.

Latona's connection to every computer and robot on the premises is definitely the biggest problem. Nesho thinks, noting her ability to communicate with not only Padraig, but command every hound and hawk on the property. *With her as the crux, Padraig has nothing to worry about, even while he's away*

"They are on their way. Please, have a seat until they arrive. Would you like anything to eat or drink in the meantime?" Latona asks, gesturing toward the dining room table.

"Do you happen to have any apple juice? I'll take a glass if you do! I've been craving it the entire drive here." Nesho requests with a smile as they pass the open living area directly to the right of the front door, and enter the dining room. Latona appears perplexed by the quick response, but walks over to the kitchen and retrieves the glass without a word.

"Master Rian was correct. You truly are impossible to predict. Most couldn't fathom a drink with such pressure looming over them, but here you are." Latona laughs warmly as she places the tall glass on the table, seeming to look for an endorsing smile from Malena before realizing she had forgotten her manners. "Oh, how rude of me to ignore your guest. Would you like anything as..."

"Nesho! Are you really here? Are you really alive?" Nesho hears bellow from across the island in the open kitchen, as the backdoor is swung open with enough force to nearly knock off the hinges.

Nesho turns his head away from the glass of juice that was mere millimeters from his lips, and beams from ear to ear. Rian starts to run around the island, over to his friend, but he is quickly restrained by Padraig's large palm, gripping at his shoulder, as the man observes with silent curiosity.

"It's me alright! Sorry for that little scare." He turns his attention to Zilch briefly, who is taken aback by the human timbre. "And no, I'm no sombra. It's the real me, with just a little cosmetic surgery." He jokes, pointing to his own radiant eyes.

Zilch rushes ahead of Padraig and Rian, and stands in front of the seated Nesho. ["What are you?"] Zilch asks, grabbing the collar of Nesho's freshly washed, platinum hoodie and lifting him to his feet. Malena's chair screeches across the floor as she rises as well.

"I don't know what I am any more than you do. I just woke up like this." Nesho explains nonchalantly. "But, could you please let go, Zilch? This is my favorite jacket, and I already had to have it cleaned once thanks to you getting blood all over it. I'd like to keep it spotless for the occasion." Nesho pleads, peering into the abyss of Zilch's eyes.

"And what occasion might that be, Nesho?" Padraig asks, caressing his chin and releasing Rian from his vice. Rian remains at his father's side awaiting the answer.

"I may be more inclined to answer once your friend lets me go." Nesho asserts, pointing to Zilch sarcastically.

"Interesting. Let him go." Padraig commands. Zilch hesitates and looks back, but concedes, taking a step back as he releases the teenager. "Now, before we really get going, I have to ask. Why did you bring a guest to my home?" Padraig questions with a devilish grin.

Nesho brushes the shoulders of his jacket and straightens the collar. "I brought Malena as proof. To show I know about your experiments, and your intentions for her." He confidently pounds his chest and looks back to Malena. "But truly, I brought her so she and Emmanuel could be freed from that fate. I want you to remove the chips from their necks and set them free, in exchange for my work in your lab."

Padraig claps with approval, giving an exhilarated nod. "Proof of your supernatural knowledge and a deal all in one. Zilch approached me in a similar fashion." He chuckles.

"He promised me an eternal being with black hair, sable eyes, and a strange voice; a creature that wore the skin of a man and held power over death, whose wit could match that of The Doctor's. That was to be proof of his own claim, of being such a creature, and a gift in good faith." Padraig reveals. "And once this 'sombra' arrived, I would release Latona from her duties, and my current projects would be sidelined to focus on the elimination of his mental affliction."

Padraig scratches his head, agitating his vermillion locks. "However, though your shared habits are undeniable, you look much more human than he described. Well, except for those glowing eyes; they make mine look so dull."

["The fact you can see those eyes is what concerns me the most, Padraig. That's why we can't allow him into your lab before we know what is going on."] Zilch cautions, fluttering his fingers as William once had.

"Even though I don't look or sound the part, I can assure you that the memories of thousands before me now reside in this head. And, as the genuine Nesho White, I was already blessed with a sharp intellect - as I'm sure Rian would attest - so, there's no doubt I will be an asset to your work." Nesho shrugs with his palms raised. *A little cockiness should appeal to the Devil.* He thinks.

The scarlet-haired genius grins lightly, obviously pleased by the show of confidence. "How about we get right to business then? Latona, could you please escort Malena to the workshop basement and have Arachne remove the chips from her and Emmanuel's necks." Padraig requests with a handwave.

"Of course, Sir. Come, Malena, let's take you back to your husband." Latona says, gesturing for Malena to follow with her hand. Malena looks to Nesho in hesitation, but Nesho grins and raises his eyebrow.

"What are you waiting on? This is what we came here for. Go see you husband, and we'll meet up when I'm done here." The confident Nesho urges.

Malena quietly concedes and follows Latona, stopping only for a moment as she passes Padraig. "One day, you will suffer for all you've done to the people of this world you've supposedly sought to make better, and on that day I'll laugh."

"I look forward to hearing you in such a jovial mood. I'm sure your laugh is quite alluring." Padraig retorts as she trails Latona out of the door.

Once the door has shut behind them, Nesho leans to the side to look at his classmate's expression. "Rian, you look so serious even though your father just took two major strides toward his goal. Has learning exactly how your father wishes to change this world with his technology given you second thoughts?" He questions, lazily pointing his finger at Padraig.

Rian looks to his father, pensive. "While I'd prefer to work in a humane fashion, my dad has already explained that helping humanity move forward without sacrifice is a childish dream. And he's probably right. Test subjects are required, and our lab has and will continue to keep that sacrifice to a minimum as we carry humanity to heights they could never have dreamt possible."

"Your father must have given you one hell of a speech for someone as kind as you to say something so cruel." Nesho looks to Zilch, who is shaking his head - most likely rejecting yet another frivolous request from Peril - and then back to Padraig and Rian.

Padraig titters at the assertion but refrains from responding.

"Yes, it is cruel, and when Zilch first told me what my dad was really doing, I couldn't imagine being a part of this. But after we spoke, Dad made me realize that once our mission succeeds, all around the world, disease, mental illness, disabilities, and physical ineptitude will be a thing of the past. Medicine, labor, and even war will be changed forever! Bringing human casualties on all fronts to new lows." Rian spews desperately, as if trying to persuade himself. "Everyone's life will be better for it, so the world will understand. One day."

Nesho laughs mockingly. "Maybe. But, if Malena is any example, I'm sure the people being sacrificed would rather live their lives than suffer at the whims of your father." He says solemnly. "That's something you'll need to accept if you're ever going to come to terms with this work. And, frankly, I don't think you can handle the weight of such a burden. You're already conflicted."

Rian balls his fist and lunges across the kitchen and into the dining room, shoving Zilch to the side with unusual force and staring death into Nesho as he hoists his curly-haired rival by the jacket's collar and threatens to punch his sly grin into oblivion. His aquamarine eyes spark and crackle like Saint Elmo's Fire, nearly chilling Nesho to the bone. But, looking past the flare of anger, Nesho sees the waves of despair crashing against the ship.

"Go ahead, if it will clear your head and help you realize your father's path isn't what's best for you. Zilch and I can handle the lab with your father, you aren't needed."

Before Rian can respond, Padraig's watch lights up, and Latona's voice rings from its speakers. "Master Padraig, the hawks have spotted a van from Armonia School approaching the home. It will reach the driveway in two minutes. Would you like me to have them intercept, sir? We can also take care of the taxi driver while we are at it."

"Fine by me, go on ahea.."

"Whoa, whoa, whoa!" Nesho protests, halting the order. "That's probably Silvie. Y'know, Ms. Lucero from Armonia. She must have tracked my phone here once she realized Malena and I snuck away from the church." Nesho pulls out the flip-phone in his pocket, waving it around to give credence to his story. "Please, let me just call her and the cabbie so I can have them go home. They have nothing to do with this, and I'm sure I can convince Silvie that Malena and I will be safe."

There was no reason for Zilch to have shared the Lucero lineage with Padraig, so all Nesho can do is hope that lack of a reason was enough for it to never have come up in conversation. "Besides, I'm sure a taxi driver won't even remember he was here after a few days. Especially if nothing strange happens."

Padraig juggles the idea, closing his eyes and bobbing his head side to side; clearly not convinced.

"Padraig, this is the woman that named me for God's sake. Please don't do it." Nesho begs once more. *Without her you'd be talking to Cornelius or Amir, instead of Nesho.* He thinks, remembering the story about Silvie's suggestion mere days before his birth as his mother, Shazmin, struggled with coming up with a name for her baby boy.

"Dad, please just let Ms. Lucero go. It's not like she can hinder your plans either way." Rian adds, releasing Nesho. The teeth of the zipper at the top of the collar appear crushed, now warped and rendered useless. "This way there's less trouble for us."

Raising his palms with a shrug, Padraig concedes. "Fair enough, Rian. You have thirty seconds. Call the overzealous nun before she gets too close, Nesho."

Nesho smiles warmly at Rian, pressing the number 1 to speed dial Silvie's phone number. "Thank you, Rian. Now, no one has to die unnecessarily." He raises the phone to his ear and, while pressing the star key on his phone, he initiates the final step of his plan. "Silvie, come on in, the defenses are down." Nesho announces as a deafening warble falls upon the home.

The metallic crash of hawks falling from the sky accompanies the pulsating roar, and Padraig's watch appears to glitch and shut off.

["I told you something was up, Padraig, you arrogant bastard!"] Zilch screams as he swivels and jets toward the back door in the kitchen, rushing to Latona's aid. The moment he exits, a fist strikes the side of Zilch's head, and the door swings shut behind him. No sounds from the back area can be heard over the overwhelming cry of the hawk that had once monitored Malena, but now obeys the commands of Nesho.

The assault on Zilch momentarily distracts Padraig as his head jerks to face the doorway, and, with opportunities sure to be far and few between, Nesho drops the phone to grab his awestruck friend's hand, pulling him toward the front door. "I don't believe for a second that you're capable of assisting in your father's madness. I still believe in the world you want to create, and I'll do anything to make it happen, even take down your father." Nesho screams as they zip past the structural wall that separates the dining room from the hall and circumvent the couch of the living area.

Nesho never looks back, nor can he hear a reply, but he takes the lack of resistance to his pull as agreement on Rian's part.

The front door flies open, revealing Silvie brandishing a revolver on the other side of the threshold. She fires past Nesho's head, and a grunt can be heard from behind him over the cry of the hawk. Nesho pushes Rian ahead of him and Silvie guides her student through the threshold with a palm at his back. "Go!" She screams at Rian before reaching for Nesho.

But, before he can reach her, Nesho sees the headlights of Padraig's blue pickup, the Adeona, charging toward Silvie's back, the sound of its tires ripping through the desert lawn disguised by the hawk's screech. That mere moment stretches into eons, and Nesho's face twists into anguish. Then, Rian's hand shoots back into sight, gripping Silvie by the arm and pulling her out of the demonic truck's path as it slams into the doorway. The front door flies past Nesho's left and he jumps back as the door frame explodes from the forceful machine barging through its frame.

Just before the pickup's grill reaches Nesho, it stops dead in its tracks, prompting Nesho to fall to his knees in relief.

A sharp whistle blares from behind Nesho, and he turns to face Padraig who stands inches behind him, applauding. "Great reflexes. Nowhere near Rian's level, but still impressive." He praises as he ends his applause and teasingly jiggles a key fob.

Nesho flashes Padraig his signature smile, in a futile attempt to pacify, just before Padraig fully grips the flowing fabric of his hood and yokes Nesho to the left. *I knew it wouldn't go so smoothly.* He thinks as he is slung across the living room. Nesho's body slams against the wall-length bookshelves, shattering his left shoulder.

Books rain down with Nesho's body, crashing to the ground around him. The stabbing, searing pain in his shoulder does all it can to usurp Nesho's thoughts. *My plan didn't involve getting injured, but they're still divided. I can still make this work.* Nesho thinks, his arm screaming as a few more fractures reveal themselves during the struggle to his feet.

Nesho looks up to Padraig, who kicks the couch aside with a quick sweep of his foot, sending it skidding across the floor until it crashes against the dining room table, causing Nesho's glass of apple juice to tip and crash onto the floor.

With his left hand, now bloodied from the wound on his wrist caused by Silvie's bullet, Padraig holds up Nesho's abandoned phone by its familiar yellow and blue antenna. "I see. Malena already had the tracker removed and you adapted it to this phone so you could control the hawk that was keeping tabs on her. The fact that the phone no longer works, and that the retrievers never attacked Ms. Lucero, means that you probably modified the jamming signal already programmed into the pursuit-model hawk so that it would emit a new frequency that can affect my creations as well. You used my own knowledge and technology against me; color me impressed, clever little sombra."

"Thanks for the compliment, but don't flatter yourself. I used Rian's memories, not yours, you damned Oulí." Nesho shouts back in response, holding his arm as blood trickles down his left index finger. *After blocking a bullet with your watch and tossing me across the room like that, I see why you weren't concerned about Malena truly hurting Rian.* He surmises. "Now, how did you get the Adeona to move, it should be jammed along with everything else."

"Well, well. Now, I know that piece of trivia could only come from me. You sombra truly are fascinating. It's been a while since I last heard the name The Doctor gave to those that survived his experiments and bear the cross-shaped marks they leave. To you, our abilities must make us seem like monsters, but, unlike you, I am still technically human. Padraig's tone is serious, but contemplative as he scans the wound on the outside of his left wrist.

"I told you, I'm not a sombra. I am still Nesho." Nesho asserts, buying himself time to regain his composure. "Now, answer me!"

"So pushy, even under the circumstances, huh?" Padraig guffaws. "Well, you're lucky I find that endearing. I took the precaution of modifying the Adeona as an extreme escape measure, once I agreed to work with Zilch and he revealed to me the depths of a sombra's knowledge; a measure to combat our shared mastery and his potential threat. The Adeona now not only operates on a different frequency than all of the other machines, but is also controlled by this fob and not my watch as it once was." Padraig admits, crushing the phone with ease and dropping the pieces to the ground as he places the fob back into the back pocket of his black dress pants.

"But, let's move on. I'm sure a creature with your knowledge can understand that my methods are the shortest way to raise up humanity; the only chance they have of snatching away the leash that The Doctor has been using to choke this world. So, explain. Why would you put yourself in my way? I'd like to hear the reason, if you'd be so kind. I'd like to know before I dissect you and augment your brain like Latona." Padraig inquires, yelling over the hawk's screech.

Nesho shuns the cries of his body and straightens his back. "Who knows? Maybe I'm just too simple to see the bigger picture." Nesho laughs, clutching his shoulder and applying pressure to keep his swaying arm still. "I just can't wrap my head around treating humans inhumanly in order to make them better. Sure, I want to help as many people as possible, but if I have to torture someone to do it, or play with their body like a toy, that's not worth it."

Nesho widens his stance, prepared to dodge his attacker's next, certain lunge. He takes in one last breath, shouting at the top of his lungs. "So, I choose Rian's childish altruism over your blood-soaked utopia! I choose to stop you for good!"

Padraig closes the distance between the two in an instant, and all Nesho can do is jump to the side as the blur of his crosshatched scars whips past him to puncture a hole through the bookcase, and into the wall behind.

Though he thanks his reflexes for the save, the thought is truncated by Padraig's left hand, gripping at his throat and lifting him up to eye level. *Why do they keep picking me up?* He bemoans, kicking violently as the thick fingers constrict his throat, with just shy of enough force to crush his larynx.

"You know that boy hates you, right? Said you're always so damn pushy and confident he can't stand it. Though, personally, that's what I've loved about our little meeting today." Padraig admits. "In any case, I have no idea what compelled him to meet you out by the library, but don't go thinking you're friends just because of that!" Padraig tightens his grip. "But maybe you'll find a friend in him once I add you to the system, though. Yes, someone as interesting as you will make a fine replacement for Latona."

Nesho lets go of his shoulder and grabs a syringe from his right pocket. *Okay, Finn, let's hope your concoction works on the Devil himself.* Nesho takes the syringe and plunges its needle deep into the bullet wound on Padraig's wrist, pressing the liquid into the injury.

Padraig's eyes shoot open as he tosses Nesho to the side, dislodging the empty syringe. "Now you're getting on my nerves." He gripes, flicking his wrist fervently as he turns to Nesho who landed on the couch. "But I'll admit, that was smart;

246

injecting me through the bullet wound when you couldn't have penetrated the skin on your own. So, what was it? Poison? A neurotoxin?"

Nesho's coughs are drowned out by the warbling as he grips the couch, struggling to sit up and regain control of his breathing.

Padraig sighs, starting his approach to the gasping Nesho. "Pathetic. Someone like you plans on changing the world with Rian, knowing The Doctor would never allow that. He has an army of oulí, just like me, at his disposal. Nowhere near as smart, but just as deadly and resilient. Even worse, his brilliance, riches, and resources go beyond your very dreams." Padraig declares, flaring his arms out as he looms over the beaten Nesho, disappointment clear in his eyes. "If you can't handle me, you'd never be able to change the world as you please. Now, tell me what you put into my body, make this easier on both of us."

At that moment, the warbling from the hawk ceases and a crash is heard on the roof. Padraig beams at the serendipity. "Well never mind, it looks like there is no need. Seems like the hawk ran out of power, probably due to your modification. Time is up for your little plan." He states, stepping past Nesho and the couch. "I'll just have Arachne analyze and counteract whatever you injected me with while Latona reactivates the hounds to hunt down your precious friends. You lose, Nesho."

Then, Padraig stops dead in his tracks, wafting his fingers slowly through the air. "What the hell did you put in me?" He asks, his voice trembling with fury as he turns to face Nesho once more.

Nesho watches as sweat beads on Padraig's forehead, and his pupils grow into large, sapphire-rimmed, black disks. "My friend calls it Apple Juice; just a taste of what humans are capable of on their own." Nesho responds, standing up and pointing to his own head, disguising the pain on his face with a smile. "It's a hallucinogen with some pretty nasty side effects. I had a friend whip it up just for you."

The Devil stomps the ground, causing the wood floor to cave and splinter around his navy-blue shoes. "I'm tired of your childish trifles, Nesho!" Padraig proclaims, wavering from side to side. "You think something like this would be enough to stop me?" He shouts, readying himself to pounce.

"Considering you'll suffer from unbearable pain and die of shock if you don't receive the second shot within five minutes, yes." Nesho says, struggling to keep his balance.

Padraig's stance relaxes "I'll die, you say?" He clarifies as a chuckle erupts from his chest. "Now that's good. Tell me, what do I have to do to receive that shot?"

"There's nothing you can do." Nesho solemnly admits, gripping his shoulder, "No matter how much I sift through the memories, no matter how much I think about it, I come to the same conclusion: if you live, the rest of us here will either die or end up as your test subjects one day. Even Rian would eventually be consumed by your obsession to topple The Doctor." Nesho grits his teeth, lamenting his hypocrisy. "You are a greater threat to this world, especially to those I care about, than The Doctor. I'm sorry, but I can't let you live."

Padraig scoffs, holding his head to keep lucid. "A greater threat than a man who could wipe away your existence on a whim? Such a compliment." His voice becomes slurred as he succumbs to the drug. "But, only I decide when I live or die now. That's the right all of these scars earned me; a right a child like you could never take."

Padraig twists around and sprints back across the dining room and leaps over the kitchen island. "The moment I reach my lab and reactivate Latona, it's all over for you!" Padraig screams as he barrels through the door.

What is he doing? Nesho panics. *He should be sedated and hallucinating at this point, how is he still so fast?*

Nesho rushes behind Padraig and dashes through the open passage, trampling the backdoor as if it were a mat to wipe his shoes. He looks to his left to see two hawks, having fallen from the sky, lying next to the pieces of a trisected hound unfortunate enough to find itself beneath them.

To his right, he sees an unconscious Zilch sprawled on the ground next to the workshop. And limping toward the incapacitated sombra is Alyssa, holding her ribs and gasping with each pained step. Alyssa's face is scuffed, but she has no major wounds to Nesho's relief. *I knew it was smart to get the Seed Trio involved.* He self-congratulates, momentarily relieved but never breaking his stride toward the doorless workshop.

Nesho sprints inside to see the door, dented and driven off its hinges, laying on the floor. To the side of the left silver table lies Latona, still shut down.

With no Padraig in sight, Nesho dashes over to the open shaft in the floor; the elevator shaft to Hell on earth. A weak voice groans from the bottom, begging for Latona's assistance.

The pleas continue in vain, and Nesho spots Malena, standing before the broken Padraig as the lights of the basement illuminate them sixty feet below.

"Latona, what are you doing? Take me to Arachne, now! I can't feel my body. Hurry!" Padraig yells between gurgles of blood.

He must have fallen and broken his neck. Nesho thinks, kneeling, helpless to do more at the shaft's edge. *Finn's drugs must have kept him from seeing that the elevator was already lowered. I guess even he couldn't survive landing on his neck from that height.*

Malena just stands there in silence; never moving a hand, never stepping away, never averting her gaze.

Eight hours had passed since Nesho beat death; two days since Malena had abandoned her village. Now, as the sun finally hides itself beyond the horizon and the stars emerge, Padraig's whimpers die out. Malena looks up to Nesho. He can't see her expression, but he is sure her cheeks are soaked with tears as she stands trembling in the Hell that had claimed not only her husband, but his killer as well.

Nesho closes his eyes, swallowing the guilt of having claimed a life, and stands up. *Evil must be slain or avoided. Evil must be slain or avoided.* He repeats in his head, reaching into his back pocket to pull out his real phone and unlocking the screen to call Silvie. "It's all clear now, you can bring Rian back."

PRISM 1: PART 3

THE FIRST WHITE LIE

NESHO WHITE

By the time Silvie arrives with Rian in tow, Malena had already raised the platform back to the workshop and wiped her tears, leaving Padraig's body on the pad like the limp body of slain prey. Silvie bolts to Nesho's side at the platform's edge to perform first aid while Rian remains standing at the threshold. He grasps his face, clawing his cheeks as he bawls at the top of his lungs. His left cheek starts to bleed from his scraping nails, and the horror in his eyes is unmistakable.

"Shut the hell up, boy! Your father was a perverted fiend that deserves no sympathy. None of your mourning, none of that damn crying." Malena chastises. "He deserved this fate for what he did to my Emmanuel!"

The verbal reprimand shakes the whole room and brings Rian's cry to an abrupt end. He turns his gaze to the hurting Malena, scorn burning behind the aquamarine glass.

"Malena. Cálmate." Silvie demands with a glacial tone, sitting between the two as she tends to Nesho. "No matter how you feel about the man, Rian still lost someone. Just like you."

Both Rian's and Malena's eyes soften slightly, though the anger behind them never fully leaves. Rian turns his head and notices Latona, and rushes to her side. "Please, please be okay." Rian begs as he reactivates the cyborg that had raised him; the earliest of many victims – kidnapped and modified around the time of Rian's birth.

Nesho sits dreary eyed as Silvie wraps up his arm, wondering what would become of Latona now that she was all Rian had left in the world. *Would he be willing to remove her limiters and set her free as Zilch requested? Should he?* He wonders, too afraid to ask Rian himself.

Relief washes over Rian's face as she powers on and greets her only remaining master.

"Master Rian, why are you crying?" She asks, wiping the teen's tears. He looks over to the body and all is immediately clear. "Oh my, Master Rian, I'm so sorry." She says, embracing and soothing the young man, until she notices the guests in the shed, and the white of her eyes shifts to black. "How would you like me to proceed with them?" She asks, hugging Rian tighter.

The whirling of machines powering up and rustling of grass can be heard as the retrievers reawaken and the rainbow sliver revolves in Latona's eyes.

Rian hugs her back tightly, being careful not to crush her. "Don't worry about them. They are only here to help." The boy commands with a whimper. "Please just stay here, I need this more than anything."

Though Nesho could feel Silvie's anxiety born from the ominous plea for orders, she is relieved by Rian's response. Nesho then assures her that with Padraig gone, there is nothing to worry about; Rian is the only one left that can command Latona, who would have no motivation to retaliate on her own.

Silence falls over the workshop as Rian and Latona continue to embrace, with only Rian's stray sobs to pierce it. With no sign of the emotional spats ending anytime soon, Alyssa and Daniel waltz in, with an incoherent and mumbling Zilch on their shoulders.

"So where do you want this guy?" Alyssa asks Nesho and Silvie, impatiently. "He won't be any trouble, since we dosed him with a seed as soon as he was knocked out, just like you asked, but he's pretty heavy."

Silvie turns to them, finishing her makeshift, blue-hoodie sling for Nesho. "He'll need to go into the cell in the basement." She pauses for a moment, considering the implications. "But that can wait until Rian is ready to move his father." She adds with as much warmth as she can muster.

Rian never acknowledges her statement, but orders Latona to go down with Alyssa and Daniel so she can place his father's body on the table.

"If she's going down, Silvia, I'll need your help retrieving Emmanuel. After all he did to try and save me, only to end up on the table with his back ripped open and half his spine torn out, replaced with Padraig's cursed machines. The least I can do is bury him as soon as possible." Malena requests of her old friend, shaken up at the thought of her husband's mutilated cadaver. "Oh God, Silvia! His eyes! His kind, brave, beautiful, chocolate eyes. I don't even know where they are, Padraig replaced them with his damn prosthetics!" She yells as she falls to her knees and cries, bringing even Rian's own sobs to a halt.

Silvie crawls over quickly to comfort her friend and agrees. "How about this? You and I will go down with Latona and get Emmanuel." She proposes, turning to Alyssa and Daniel. "To keep the platform from being too crowded, we'll have you wait up here until we return. Then, Alyssa, you and Daniel can carry Zilch to the holding cell. Does that sound good to everyone?"

Both Rian and Alyssa are quick to agree, both seeing no other options, though most likely for different reasons. Silvie's presence and voice still clearly intimidates Alyssa, leaving her quick to comply - hoping to end any conversation with the pastor's assistant swiftly - but Rian seems to simply wish to be finished with the entire ordeal. Nesho gets up and walks to where Rian is sitting on the floor, his cheeks still flushed with tears and his eyes bloodshot, and takes a seat next to him without saying a word.

The swapping and placing of bodies takes about fifteen, deadly-quiet minutes before all is said and done, and after Latona helps Emmanuel's body into the nearly indestructible Adeona to be transferred to Armonia for burial, it is Zilch's turn to be moved to the basement.

Sorry, Zilch. Nesho thinks as he watches the platform descend into the subterranean lab with Latona, Alyssa, Daniel, and Zilch. *But we don't know if you'll be a danger once you wake up fully. I'm sure that between Finn and I, we can develop something to end your visions of Peril for good. Just wait until then.* Nesho feels no better than Padraig by planning to lock away the sombra indefinitely, but he knows the combination of Padraig's knowledge and Peril's madness is too dangerous to unleash upon the world. *Free of Peril, you could become an even greater blessing to humanity than Dara Lucero.* Nesho proposes silently.

After another five minutes of excruciating, dead silence passes, during which Rian seemed just as reluctant to speak as Nesho while both Malena and Silvie remained outside to discuss next steps, the platform finally returns to the top of the workshop with no Zilch in sight.

Alyssa and Daniel exit the workshop, while Rian moves over to Latona's side and sits in the chair, facing the computer.

Nesho keeps to himself on the side, though he slightly overhears the separate conversations between Silvie and Malena, and Alyssa and Daniel outside as he watches Rian stare at the blank screen with Latona at his side, awaiting her next order. Silvie and Malena plan to check on their village in the coming days, once they were certain Nesho was in the clear and safe with his mother, while Alyssa and Daniel discuss the monster of a man that rammed through two doors and experimented on people in his basement.

"Even if we were blackmailed into helping, I'm glad Finn decided to cave and work with them, instead of skipping town again. I can't imagine the sick experiments that Padraig guy was conducting down there." Daniel whispers.

"He probably just would have run if it weren't for you always buzzing in his ear. Then there's the deal they made that will make improving the seeds easier." Alyssa points out, exhaustion heavy in her voice. "So, it's not like he had no incentives. In any case, if we are all squared away here, I'm ready to get back so we can report to Finn and go to bed. It's been a rough two days."

"Ahh Alyssa, before you go…" Silvie interjects sternly. "Here is your father's gun back. I would like to thank you two; we couldn't have done this without you. Successfully neutralizing Zilch is the only thing that made this victory possible."

"I wish I could take credit for that, but he honestly beat me to a pulp; every single throw, every single strike, he threw them back in my face like it was nothing." Alyssa pauses, gritting her teeth as she places her father's gun in her jacket's inner pocket. "Even worse, he criticized my habits and weaknesses like he'd watched me train in Judo my entire life, all while ordering me to leave with Daniel before we become needless casualties. I was only able to get one hit on him when he was muttering something to himself. He barely took a step back. Just thanked me for 'shutting that damned mask up.'"

Alyssa rubs the back of her head, as if embarrassed by her own futile efforts. "If it wasn't for Padraig knocking Zilch to the side when he burst out of that back door, that black-haired monster would have probably knocked me unconscious."

"I see." Silvie's voice softens slightly as she seems to envision her student's despairing bout. "Even still, your efforts were noble, and I'm glad everything worked out. But remember, you three are on thin ice. Nesho may have no worries about you, but I will be watching to make sure you all never stray from the straight and narrow. At least, until you all redeem yourselves."

"Is that really what you are concerned about right now? I only did what I did because Jacob…" Alyssa grunts as a muddled thwack interrupts her.

"We understand, Ms. Lucero. Believe me, no one wants to redeem themselves more than us. We'll earn your trust, even Finn, as long as I'm around." Daniel says, each word free of doubt.

"Glad to hear it, Daniel. You all are free to go. Tell Finn that we will be in contact as soon as we get the resources to help in his research. And Ms. Garcia, I'll see you on Monday." Silvie says.

"Of course." Alyssa replies begrudgingly.

Nesho can hear the footsteps of Alyssa and Daniel grow quiet as they meander toward the front of the house, back to Daniel's cab.

"Did you want to ride in the trunk again?" Daniel asks with a jokey tone, clearly trying to brighten the mood.

"Hah, hah. Very funny, Daniel." Alyssa responds, just as their voices become too distant for Nesho to make out another word.

"So, are you ever going to say anything?" Nesho hears Rian question as he swivels his chair to face his mute classmate.

"I don't know what to say." Nesho replies honestly. "I thought stopping your father and saving as many people as possible would feel good, but I just feel sick."

The workshop returns to a brief silence as Nesho searches for the words to better explain his feelings, but Rian is the first to break it with genuine warmth. "Thanks, Nesho."

Shocked, Nesho raises his head to see a smiling Rian walking toward him and extending his hand. "What?"

"I said 'thank you.'" The red-head repeats. "Everyone else here is only talking about my dad as a monster, but you feel bad, even if it's just for me. Even though he was beyond saving, he is still my dad. So, I'm grateful that someone isn't celebrating."

Nesho takes Rian's hand and accepts his helpful lift up to his feet. "So, how much did Zilch tell you?"

"Everything, I think. That my dad and I aren't descended from the Celts like I thought, we're not even human. That doppelgangers are real, and you call them brillos and sombras. That Lati isn't an android, but a cyborg built around a woman he kidnapped when I was born. That my dad had been experimenting on nearly two hundred people, right beneath my feet." Rian turns toward the computer desk, hiding the depths below. "I just can't believe it. I spent my entire life building and learning in this shop, trying to improve so I could help my dad change the world, just to find out people were suffering sixty feet below us. That the prosthetics I helped design were being used on unwilling lab rats."

Nesho grabs his friend's shoulder, trying to comfort the teen whose world had changed more than anyone's in a mere eight hours. "I'm so sor.."

"Don't you dare apologize!" Rian yells, provoking Silvie and Malena to run back inside. "Just tell me what I have to do to make all of this worth it." He begs, with tears welling up in his eyes.

Nesho looks over to the computer and points to the keyboard. "You have to take your father's place, and work under The Doctor." *It's the only way we can avoid The Doctor's retaliation. We aren't ready to tackle him quite yet.*

"Won't that require me to become just like him?" A shocked Rian exclaims.

"No, your father had free reign over his experiments and methods, as long as he also developed tech that would be useful for The Doctor's *Davy-Swan* company." Nesho assures. "And since he is already aware your father had you work alongside him in the upper level, The Doctor will most likely accept your offer to replace him out of convenience."

"Understood, but won't he be suspicious that I was involved in my father's death?" Rian wonders aloud.

"Of course. That's why you'll need to take the blame for it right off the bat." Nesho states, rubbing his head out of guilt. "Just tell him about the deal he made with Malena, and claim she came to you instead and begged you to put an end to your father so she could rescue her husband. Tell him that, together, you foiled his evil plots forever by drugging and pushing him down the shaft. Then, after saving her husband, Malena left without a trace; the rest of us were never here."

"And under no circumstance can he find out about La Sombra in the cage." Silvie quickly chimes.

"That makes sense. From how my father and Zilch described him, The Doctor would have everyone even remotely related to what happened today killed if he found out a sombra, like himself, was involved." Rian responds, his voice glum as he accepts his heavy role as deceiver and returns to his seat at the desk. "So, should I just make the call now? While everything is still fresh? That'll make it more believable, right?"

"I...I guess. But are you sure you don't want to wait? We can stay for a bit longer if you need us." Nesho offers, hesitant to leave Rian alone so soon.

"It's okay. You need to get your arm checked out anyway." Rian states, turning the computer on without looking back to Nesho or the group. "We'll need you in tip-top shape if we really want to make the world a better place together."

Nesho smiles lightly, still unsure if leaving is the right choice. Then, he feels Silvie's slender hand grip his good shoulder. "If that is what you wish, Rian, we will leave you for now. But remember, you are always part of Armonia, and we will always be there for you if you need us." The administrator affirms with a gentle tone.

"I know. Thanks." Rian replies, never turning to face her.

After a brief silence, both Silvie and Malena step out of the workshop. Hesitantly, Nesho follows as Latona bows and wishes them a safe trip.

The mission was a success; it was finally over. But Nesho still can't leave. Not like this. So, just before passing the threshold, he stops.

"Do you think we'd get in trouble if we skipped school Monday for your birthday?" Nesho asks, hoping to leave his friend with a bit of light in the bleak workshop. "Though I'm sure Ms. Hughes would tear us a new one for not finishing our world civilizations project on time." He jokes.

Rian titters at the reminder of the project whose topic he demanded to change just yesterday. "Just come up with a good excuse, and I'm sure we'll get an extension. I'm sure your arm will do the trick."

"Yeah I guess you're right." Nesho chuckles lightly, before stepping into the backyard and leaving Rian behind as Latona bows him goodbye.

Once they get to the Armonia van, Silvie tells him they are going to see Dr. Renner after they drop off Malena and Emmanuel at the church. As the Adeona trails them during their return, Nesho falls asleep in the backseat, exhausted from his transformative Saturday.

During his sleep, he dreams of himself as a young, Caucasian boy dressed in a gray jumpsuit. Before him, is a glass wall with a singular metal tube, no wider than a hand, that leads inside. Its sealed end opens, revealing a set of inner, silicon curtains.

Nesho feels his hands forced into the tube, and he witnesses hundreds of giant mosquitos, with three-inch long wings, flock to his arm, and bite him in unison. He tries to jerk his arm out, but the force keeping his arm in the hole won't relieve him. Each bite stings like a flaming whip, his skin getting hotter with each blow as he feels his blood bubble underneath. The heat travels through his body until his entire being feels like it may explode; until finally he feels the skin on his arm do just that.

Nesho, finally able to pull out, falls onto his back with a shrill screech that destroys his own vocal cords. He looks up to see the one who was holding his arm into the hole is, none other than, The Doctor himself. His triangle sunglasses block his eyes, but the depth of his glee is quickly betrayed by the menacing curve of his lips as it pushes away his thick beard to reveal his teeth.

Before Nesho can question what is going on, he is woken by Silvia's voice. "Nesho! Are you okay?" She questions from the driver's seat once she sees his eyes open. "I think you were having a nightmare."

"Sí mija, todo va bien. No te preocupes." Nesho replies as a cold sweat drips down his back and his arm continues to pulse with pain.

Silvia focuses on Nesho through the rearview mirror as Malena turns around to look as well. "Mija? Are you sure you're okay, Nesho?" Silvia asks.

Just as Nesho realizes what he said, his right arm tenses further, forcing the shape of his hand into a twisted claw. The pain, like searing wounds that bore through his flesh, makes no sense to the boy as he scans his uninjured arm. Then, his breathing shallows, comprehending that the foreign memories must be leaching into his mind against his will and affecting his perception of the world.

For only an instant, Nesho considers telling Silvia about the dream in detail and the visceral feeling it left in his arm, but he shrugs it off. *She has enough to worry about. I can handle this if the sombra can.*

"Sorry, Silvia." He says while hiding his right hand between his knees. "I'm fine. Just had a bad dream."

PATIENT BLACK TENOR
FREEZE THE SNOWDROPS AND BIRDSONG
PLAY YOUR WINTER'S DIRGE

SPANISH GLOSSARY

PRISM 7

1) ¿Qué pasó? || What's wrong? (8)

2) No puedo mover las piernas o los brazos. || I can't move my legs or arms. (8)

3) No me los puedo sentir. || I can't feel them. (8)

4) Debe de ser el hijo del diablo. || He must be that devil's son. (9)

5) Si lo hubiera atrapado, podría haberla rescatado. || If I would have captured him, I could have saved her. (9)

6) ¿Adónde me lleva? || Where are you taking me? (11)

7) ¿Qué demonios? || What the hell? (12)

8) Mi vida. || My love/My life (12)

9) Debes estar aquí. || You must be here. (12)

10) He venido al infierno. || I've come to hell. (13)

11) Pero, lo haría mil veces, si pudiera rescatarla. || But I would do it a thousand times if I could rescue her. (13)

12) Malena, lo siento mi vida. ‖ Malena, I'm sorry my love. (14)

13) Todo esto es culpa mía. ‖ All of this is my fault. (14)

14) Nada es culpa tuya, viejo. ‖ Nothing is your fault, sweetheart. (15)

15) Todo va a salir bien, ya verás. No te preocupes. ‖ Everything is going to turn out fine, you'll see. Don't worry. (15)

16) Qué locura. ‖ How absurd/How crazy (16)

17) ¿Qué tiene que ver? ‖ What does that have to do with anything? (16)

18) ¡Menos mal! ‖ Thank God! (Not literal) (17)

19) Lo que estoy a punto de pedirte es muy importante. ¿mejor que hable español, yo? ‖ What I am about to ask you is very important. Is it better that I speak Spanish? (18)

20) Lo mataré, viejo. ‖ I will kill him, sweetheart. (21)

PRISM 6:

1) Hada ‖ Pronunciation: Ah-duh ‖ Fairy (35)

2) Jacaranda ‖ Pronunciation: Hah-kah-rahn-duh (40)

3) ¿Qué tienes ahora? ‖ What do you have now?

4) El hada más linda de Chula Vista. ‖ The most beautiful fairy of Chula Vista (48)

PRISM 5:

1) Te quiero mija. ‖ I love you, my daughter (96)

2) Te quiero papa. ‖ I love you, Papa. (96)

PRISM 3:

1) El Brillo ‖ Pronunciation: Bree-yo ‖ Name of the larval form of the memory snatching creature. Translates to The Shine. (141)

2) Curandera ‖ Medicine Woman (146)

3) Dos Ojos ‖ Name of Silvia and Malena's home village. Translates to Two Eyes. (146)

4) La de Las Vendajes ‖ Woman of the Black Bandages (149)

5) Banda ‖ Gang (149)

6) ¡Querida, escóndete! ‖ Sweetheart, hide! (150)

7) ¿Todo va bien? ‖ Is everything okay? (152)

8) Sí, Sí ‖ Yes, yes (152)

9) Mira, antes de ir al hospital, hay algo que no entiendo. ‖ Hey look, before going to the hospital, there's something I don't understand. (152)

10) ¿Para qué te dejó viva ese Padraig? ¿Te dijo, Malena? ‖ Why did that Padraig leave you alive? Did he tell you, Malena? (152)

11) ¿Por qué te importa ahora? ‖ Why does it matter to you now? (153)

12) Hace unos minutos estabas lista para lidiar con este Padraig y sus demonios. ‖ Just a few minutes ago you were ready to deal with this Padraig and his demons. (153)

13) Para ayudarme con este dispositivo en el cuello y salvar a Emmanuel. ‖ To help me with this device in my neck and save Emmanuel. (153)

14) Sí, pero en el caos debía haber algo de ti que le llamó la atención. ‖ Yes, but in the chaos there must have been something about you that called his attention. (153)

15) Ya que, en el principio, quería operarte el ojo y no a Emmanuel. || Since, in the beginning, he wanted to operate on your eye and not Emmanuel's. (153)

16) Pero, Malena, como te dije, deberíamos hablar inglés. || But, Malena, like I told you, we should speak English. (153)

17) Los Viejos || The Elderly (158)

18) Bisabuelos || The Grandparents (158)

19) La Sombra || Pronunciation: Sohm-bruh || Name of the mature form of the memory snatching creature that has now taken over its host's body. Translates to The Shadow. (160)

20) Ese hijo de puta. || That son of a bitch. (172)

21) ¿Qué pasa, Silvia? || What's wrong, Silvia? (172)

22) No fue para tanto. || It wasn't a big deal. (173)

23) Casi me mataste, bruja fría. || You almost killed me, cold witch. (173)

24) ¿Silvia, de qué se trata eso? || What is that about, Silvia? (178)

25) No mames. || You have to be messing with me (vulgar) (179)

PRISM 1:

1) Cálmate. || Calm down. (254)

2) Sí mija, todo va bien. || Yes, my daughter. Everything is fine.

   (265)

3) No te preocupes. || Don't worry. (265)

TO BE CONTINUED IN BOOK 2 OF THE FIRST
WHITE LIE SERIES:

THE DOCTOR WILL
SEE YOU NOW